With knees gone unch... ...
Sophie managed to take the two steps to reach
Duane, and leaned forward to kiss him.

Long.

And again.

Her mouth opened, her tongue meeting his,
and she didn't want to let go, to break away
from this perfect moment.

Time, society, ages, past mistakes and bulimia
all faded away, leaving only what mattered
most, what would go with her into the next
life—her heart. And the heart to which hers was
irrevocably attached.

"I missed you," she said, finally pulling back far
enough to reconnect with those deep chocolate
eyes that could look at her with such warmth.

"Here." Duane held out her glass, the smile on
his lips completely genuine. "Here's to you
coming home to me."

Dear Reader,

Welcome to Shelter Valley! For those of you who've never been here before, I think you'll like your stay with us. For those of you who were here before—several years ago—welcome home!

Shelter Valley is a town—and a small one at that. It's in the desert in Arizona about an hour's drive from Phoenix. The only thing of any renown in the town is its university—Montford. The school is small, but students come from around the country to get a Montford education. They call it the Harvard of the West.

Many moons ago (there are a lot of Indian influences in Shelter Valley) Sophie Curtis was a student at Montford—hailing from Denver, Colorado, on a full scholarship. She's all grown up now. Has a successful career. And when she's not traveling, she still calls Shelter Valley home.

Sophie had some issues in college. For one, she was in love with her professor. She was certain he was in love with her, too. And told people so. Only to find out that he wasn't. As it turned out, that was the least of her problems. But Sophie's older now. Wiser.

But are we ever old enough to be fully wise?

I'm guessing probably not. But here's what I know—Shelter Valley is the place to be when you're having unwise moments. It's the place to be when you're struggling. It's the place to be when the life you were so certain was the right one for you falls into little pieces around your feet. Because in Shelter Valley people care.

Please join us.

Tara Taylor Quinn

P.S. I love to hear from readers! You can reach me at staff@tarataylorquinn.com, or at P.O. Box 13584, Mesa, AZ 85216.

TARA TAYLOR QUINN
Sophie's Secret

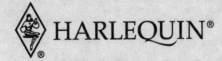

TORONTO • NEW YORK • LONDON
AMSTERDAM • PARIS • SYDNEY • HAMBURG
STOCKHOLM • ATHENS • TOKYO • MILAN • MADRID
PRAGUE • WARSAW • BUDAPEST • AUCKLAND

Recycling programs
for this product may
not exist in your area.

ISBN-13: 978-0-373-71550-3
ISBN-10:   0-373-71550-1

SOPHIE'S SECRET

Copyright © 2009 by Tara Taylor Quinn.

ABOUT THE AUTHOR

With more than forty-five original novels, published in more than twenty languages, Tara Taylor Quinn is a *USA TODAY* bestselling author with over six million copies sold. She is known for delivering deeply emotional and psychologically astute novels. Ms. Quinn is a three-time finalist for the RWA RITA® Award, a multiple finalist for the National Reader's Choice Award, the Reviewer's Choice Award, the Bookseller's Best Award and the Holt Medallion. Ms. Quinn recently married her college sweetheart, and the couple currently lives in Ohio with two very demanding and spoiled bosses: four-pound Taylor Marie and fifteen-pound rescue mutt/cockapoo Jerry. When she's not writing for Harlequin and MIRA Books or fulfilling speaking engagements, Ms. Quinn loves to travel with her husband, stopping wherever the spirit takes them. They've been spotted in casinos and quaint little small-town antiques shops all across the country.

Books by Tara Taylor Quinn

HARLEQUIN SUPERROMANCE

1272–SOMEBODY'S BABY*
1297–25 YEARS
   "Best Friends"
1309–THE PROMISE
   OF CHRISTMAS
1350–A CHILD'S WISH
1381–MERRY CHRISTMAS, BABIES
1428–SARA'S SON
1446–THE BABY GAMBLE**
1465–THE VALENTINE GIFT
   "Valentine's Daughters"
1500–TRUSTING RYAN
1527–THE HOLIDAY VISITOR

*Shelter Valley Stories
**Texas Hold 'Em

MIRA BOOKS

WHERE THE
   ROAD ENDS
STREET SMART
HIDDEN
IN PLAIN SIGHT
BEHIND CLOSED
   DOORS

HARLEQUIN EVERLASTING LOVE

THE NIGHT WE MET

HARLEQUIN SINGLE TITLE

SHELTERED IN
   HIS ARMS*

For the three penguins:
we know who we are and we know what we do.
In this life and beyond.

CHAPTER ONE

"Go, 344. Go 345." Sophie Curtis spoke sotto voce into the microphone protruding from the headpiece she wore. She stood in the pitch-black area left of stage, reading the sheet on the podium by a penlight. Just three more cues and…

"Fade lights. Go curtain." The heavy, velveteen drape slid quickly down.

Dancers, singers and actors scrambled, bumping into each other, cursing, mumbling, then, three seconds later, fell into place, a perfect shape of bodies and colors, all smiles and glitter and…

"Go lights. Go curtain."

Applause thundered through the large, Midwestern university theater, the crowd at this January fund-raiser growing louder with each carefully choreographed bow. The sound rumbled inside her. Like bilious waves on a rocky sea.

The applause reached excruciating heights when Damon Adrian, off Broadway's newest heartthrob—a sure star for the silver screen—stepped forward.

One minute. Two. And then…

"Go curtain. Go house lights."

Sophie pulled off her headset, dropped it on the podium, then desperately pushed her way through the throng of moving bodies high on adrenaline. Pushed all the way through the dancers' dressing room, to the restroom then to the farthest stall.

Where she promptly threw up.

FUNNY HOW BATHROOM TILE all looked the same. Did the world have an agreement—everyone use the same tile so people would immediately recognize the place for what it was? Feel at home there? Or was it simply the cheapest flooring material that could withstand public use?

This stuff needed to be re-grouted. But then—

"Soph?"

Recognizing her friend's voice, Sophie grabbed some toilet paper, wiped her mouth again—then pulled another wad for her eyes—and stood. Prayed she was done.

"Yeah?"

"Hey." There was a tap on the stall door. Annie's blue-tipped tennis shoes, her strong dancer's ankles, were planted on the other side. "You okay?"

"Yeah." Sophie swallowed. "I'm fine."

But she wasn't. She was scared to death. And as soon as Annie saw her face, she'd know it.

"Soph? Open the door."

Déjà vu. Like old times. Sophie had thought she was done with all that. Had confidently told Annie so just the night before.

"Sophie…"

How concern and authority could blend so painfully in one word, Sophie didn't know. Had never known.

But she recognized the tone as though she was still that twenty-year-old undergrad at Montford University in Shelter Valley, Arizona, rather than the twenty-eight-year-old successful theatrical producer she'd become.

Like that twenty-year-old she'd once been, she opened the door. And couldn't meet her friend's eyes.

How many times, during those years of doing shows together—Annie as a dance major and Sophie majoring in theater production—had she had to face her friend on the other side of a stall door?

"Oh, Soph. You said you were done with all that. That it had been years—"

She glanced up. "It has been."

"Show me your finger."

Sophie's long nails were legendary, though they were shorter now than they had been in college, and the bold colors they used to be adorned with had toned down to pale pinks. She held out her right palm—middle finger extended straight up.

"It's not broken off." For years the nail of that finger had been a short stub necessitated by Sophie's addiction to sticking it down her throat. Tonight, it was even with the rest—an eighth of an inch beyond her fingertip.

"I know."

"So…"

"I didn't consciously do it," Sophie said, fighting panic—and myriad other emotions that were what got her into trouble in the first place. And every place after that, as well.

If she could keep the different parts of herself neatly packed away in their respective compartments, she'd be fine. It was only when the emotions took over, spilled over, that she had problems.

They hadn't spilled over in years.

"I…really… I didn't know what was happening." At least not that she'd been able to acknowledge to herself.

She wanted to go home.

To lock herself inside her two-bedroom stucco abode on her acre of desert and sleep until she was better.

Frowning, Annie grabbed Sophie's still-extended finger, holding on. "So you didn't do it to yourself? You have the flu?"

One shouldn't sound quite so happy at the possibility that one's friend was sick.

Sophie couldn't answer.

"Soph?"

"It didn't feel like the flu," she finally admitted.

"You were able to control it," Annie said, knowing the signs, having gone through all the symptoms with Sophie the first time. "Your thoughts made it happen."

When she'd been distracted with the show, the nausea had gone away. Did that count?

Sophie could have said the words aloud, but she knew the answer. Yes, it counted.

"I brought it on myself."

Which was ridiculous. Most particularly here—at a show. Here she was a successful, confident woman. Period.

With Phyllis, her Shelter Valley friend and onetime counselor, Sophie could let the little girl inside come to the surface. Maybe. If she had to.

"Ah, Soph, I thought things were great. These past two weeks, working on the show, you've seemed so happy. Why didn't you say something? We could have taken time away, really talked."

Why hadn't she said something? Why hadn't she told her friend the whole truth? Why hadn't she told Annie— someone who'd known her before, who would under- stand—that she was struggling? Why hadn't she admitted, even silently, that she'd allowed herself to return to a place she'd vowed never to revisit?

Bulimia-ville.

"I didn't know." Sophie answered her own last question first. "I swear, Annie, this is the first time. And it really wasn't a conscious choice. I just… I guess old habits really do die hard. Or don't ever die. They just lie there, waiting to attack you when you're at a weak point."

"You know the signs, Soph. The symptoms."

Nodding, Sophie thought over the past few months. The past two years. When her sexual being had come back to life.

She thought of Duane. And quickly shut that mental door.

"I didn't see it coming," she said. "I'm older. Successful. I have many reasons to feel good about myself. I really thought I wasn't susceptible anymore."

Another dancer, a guest performer in the evening's closing performance, pushed through the door from the dressing room, said, "Sorry, I gotta pee," then, with a smile in their direction, dashed into a stall.

"Let's go find a place to get something to eat," Annie said, pulling Sophie in the direction of the door.

"You've got a cast party to get to." She'd been here two weeks and had managed to avoid any one-on-one personal conversation with the woman who'd once been such a close confidant. "And I really should hang around while they tear things down."

"The local techies are going to get all of that." Annie pointed out what they both knew. "And you've got time to finish up paperwork in the morning before your flight back to Phoenix."

Sophie allowed herself to be pulled into the bustle of a quickly emptying dressing room. "But your party—"

"Is nothing compared to you," Annie said softly. She approached her seat at the long, lighted dressing table, throwing things in her bag with an unusual disregard to orderliness. "It's not like I haven't performed with these people before, or like I won't again."

Sophie went to collect her things.

LIFTING HIS GLASS, Duane peered at the small, select group of men and women gathered in the living room of his Phoenix high-rise condo. The party was unofficial. A Saturday-night get-together of friends.

The friends just happened to be the most powerful political movers and shakers in the state of Arizona.

"You're the one, buddy," Robert Anvil said, touching his glass to Duane's as the rest of the small group nodded.

Looking to Will Parsons, the one man in the room he truly trusted, one of the few people in the world he considered a friend, Duane waited. And only drank when he received Will's quiet nod.

Any other evening he and Will got together it was at Will's home in Shelter Valley, a small town an hour's drive from Phoenix. Shelter Valley had been home to Will Parsons all his life, and a regular stopping place for Duane the past two years.

The two men had met in college—at Montford University, the Harvard of the West. Will was now president of the renowned educational institution. His wife, Becca, standing next to him tonight, was mayor of Shelter Valley.

Neither of those facts was the reason Duane considered them friends.

Toast completed, talk broke out among the twenty people who'd come together to informally offer Duane their party's nomination for the senate seat in Arizona's state election the following fall.

Relief seemed to suffuse the room, as though blown from the heating duct. Relief and anticipation, judging by the buzz of conversations Duane was catching. They'd made a good choice. Or seemed to think they had.

Duane wasn't so sure.

"You don't look like a man who's in the process of re-alizing his greatest lifetime goal."

Turning, Duane grimaced at Will, who'd maneuvered them into a corner of the room where they could speak without being overheard.

"I can do this job." Hands in his pockets, Duane looked his friend straight in the eye. "After twenty years of applying the laws in this state, I know where we need changes, and how to go about getting them. I know our weak points and our strengths—"

"Yeah." Will might be a fifty-something university president, but he was also a very involved father—one child five and another one eight—and more and more his vocabulary was relaxing.

"I just…"

"You're worried about Sophie."

Duane's eighteen-years-younger-than-him girlfriend was no secret between the two men. She was the reason for his frequent visits to Shelter Valley.

She'd been a student at Will's school not all that many years ago.

"You know as well as I do that half the people in this room would change their minds about backing me if they knew about her," Duane said.

His relationship with Sophie didn't come to Phoenix.

"When's the last time you asked her to marry you?"

"Before she left for Chicago." Two weeks ago.

"And she turned you down?"

"Of course."

Will, the only man in the room wearing a suit jacket, sipped from his glass of soda water. He rarely drank these days—one of the many changes that had accompanied Bethany's advent into his and Becca's lives when, after twenty-plus years of trying, they found out Becca was finally going to have a baby.

"Better be careful, man," Will said. "She might surprise you one of these times and accept."

Now there was a thought. One that brought more reservations than the party decision to back him.

Will's eyes narrowed. "What would you do if she did?"

"I honestly don't know."

"Maybe you'd better figure that out before you pose the question again."

It sounded so easy.

With a quick glance over his shoulder at the men and women milling behind them, Will asked, "Do you love her?"

"You know I do."

"I know you're attracted to her. That's a far cry from loving her."

"Give me a break, man. I'm forty-six, not fourteen. And it's been two years. It's more than just lust."

"So could you picture yourself spending the rest of your life with her?"

Who knew answers to such questions?

"I can picture myself at sixty, when she's forty-two. In my mind, Sophie is full of energy and beauty and bored with me."

"You don't trust her."

"It's more than that, Will. I love my time with her, crave more time with her. But when we're together we're alone. The rest of the world, and things like generations, don't matter. Can you honestly picture her here tonight? Hell, these guys would think she's my daughter. Or they'd look at her like she's on the hunt for a sugar daddy."

Will seemed to commiserate with his chuckle.

"You don't hold too high an opinion of the moral composition of our peers."

Duane took in the room, the casually dressed men and women, and saw them for what they were. Intelligent, confident, successful. Many of them would do whatever it took to get where they were going. Use who they could. Stab who they had to. Some were quick to judge each other, while justifying, at least to themselves, their own sometimes questionable actions—and would blame others if someone got hurt.

He didn't want to join the crowd. He simply wanted to change the world.

"I don't want to make Sophie look like a whore." He and Will talked straight. Which was one of the reasons Duane valued the friendship so much.

"Marrying her won't do that."

Whereas visiting her warm and vibrant home, leaving his car parked outside all night, did.

"And that's not really the problem, is it?" Will asked softly, moving them a little farther away from the others.

"You of all people know her past, Will." In his official capacity, Will had been apprised of the troubles of one of Montford's most promising scholarship students. The invitations she'd offered to too many guys—including one of her instructors. The eating disorder that had almost killed her.

"It bothers you."

"How could it not?"

"So you don't trust her."

"I don't know." Downing his Scotch, Duane turned away from a love life he couldn't control, and stepped back into the persona he'd grown comfortable with over the years. The intelligent, confident, successful attorney who'd worked his entire life for this chance to make a difference. And who really believed he could.

Make a difference, that was.

CHAPTER TWO

"OKAY, SPILL IT." The Chicago pub's late-Saturday-night crowd was the perfect size to allow Annie and Sophie to have a real conversation in privacy. Unfortunately.

Sophie wasn't into comfy and cozy conversation. She wasn't a kid anymore.

They had just shared a juicy hamburger, three quarters of which Annie made Sophie eat. She'd refused to do anything but encourage and watch until she'd witnessed Sophie chew and swallow every bite.

"I haven't had a hamburger in ages."

"And it was good, wasn't it?"

"Yeah." But the weight she instantly felt on her hips wasn't. Duane might not be so attracted to a hippopotamus.

"So if it's been ages since you've had a burger, does that mean there's been no bingeing?"

Scared at the recurrence of an illness she'd struggled so hard to beat, yet still falling prey to its symptoms, to feeling guilty for having consumed so much fat, Sophie shook her head. "None. I told you, I didn't see any obvious signs."

"So you haven't been restricting your diet?"

Translation: not eating.

"I've been busy."

"So you *have* been missing meals."

"Some." Theater work, making everything perfect in the two-day or two-week span allotted to them per show, wrought more tasks than hours in a day. And she could get twice as much accomplished during meal breaks, when the stage was empty.

Annie's disappointed look didn't weigh as heavily as the beef Sophie had consumed, confirming her fears that she'd fallen back to a day she'd promised herself she'd never see again.

She was feeling bad about herself for eating. And eating was necessary to sustain life.

"How many?" Annie's question wasn't a surprise.

Sophie glanced up, once again facing the truth of her weakness. "Too many," she admitted as she thought back over the past weeks. She'd been careful not to eat. Hadn't had a real meal since she'd arrived in Chicago. "I feel good, emotionally, when I don't eat. Like I'm doing myself a great favor, you know? I'm strong enough to beat base appetites. I'm in control—"

She sounded like the pamphlets and books she'd read.

But she wasn't speaking from them. Not eating truly gave her a sense of strength. Of control. Of power.

"There's been no weight fluctuation outside of a five-pound range," she offered softly. She'd been watching—weighing herself in the hotel workout facility. She cared.

And was determined to remain in control.

Of course, weighing yourself all the time was a symptom, too.

"What's got you so down this time, Soph? You have a home you love, in a town you love and are incredibly successful in a career you love—" Annie broke off, eyeing her steadily. "It's a man, isn't it?"

Duane's face came clearly into view, transposed upon Annie's sweet, concerned features. "Maybe."

"So is there someone serious? You haven't mentioned anyone in years, other than that Duane guy who helped you with your LLC articles of incorporation. You said you two were just friends."

Sophie had forgotten she'd told Annie anything about Duane.

And Annie had it right. She and Duane were just friends. All they ever could be. Friends who happened to sleep together. Several nights a week. But that was their business.

"No, there's no one serious." Serious meant a future. It meant a life together. And that definitely was not what she had with Duane.

Annie's face, naked as it always was when not caked with stage makeup, struck a familiar chord—reminding Sophie of a day when she'd poured out her heart.

She'd been such a pathetically weak little thing back then. It hurt to even think of that girl. Hurt more to think of the things she'd done.

"What's wrong then?" Annie asked. "Surely you aren't feeling bad about yourself for being unattached. My gosh, you're only twenty-eight, Soph. You have your whole life ahead of you. And you and I both know you could have had any number of guys if you wanted to settle down to a family right away."

Sophie shook her head. She'd changed a lot since Annie had known her. Gained confidence over the years, making choices she could be proud of.

So why did she feel like that lost twenty-year-old kid again?

"I'm in love with Duane." She couldn't believe she'd said that. Her feelings for him were her business. And his.

"Oh!" If Annie was hurt by the fact that Sophie hadn't confessed about her love life, she didn't let it show. "And he just wants to be friends? Did you tell him how you feel? I'd find it hard to believe that he doesn't love you back." As though everyone would have to love Sophie.

"He says he loves me."

"So what's the problem?"

"Problems," Sophie said. "Plural." She hesitated. Speaking about Duane felt wrong. Maybe even disloyal. Duane and Annie occupied two completely separate parts of her life.

"Soph?"

"I don't know what to say."

"You're in danger of falling back into a huge psychological health risk." Annie's voice was brisk. Firm. "Talk or you could die."

Sophie couldn't help the smile that spread across her face. And grew larger as Annie grinned, as well.

"I never claimed to be undramatic," she said.

"And exaggerative."

"That, too. But the point is—"

"I got the point. I already had it. And you're right. I'm apparently not handling things as successfully as I thought I was."

Or maybe they'd escalated to the stage that something had to be done. Which might be what was scaring her. If she and Duane couldn't continue as they had, where did that leave them?

Annie's smile faded and she leaned across the cleared table. "Tell me what's going on."

Taking a deep breath, Sophie glanced up. "Duane's forty-six."

"Oh," Annie said again. A little less enthusiastically this time.

"That's almost twenty years older than us."

"I might have a degree in dance, but I do know how to add."

"He's old enough to be my father."

"I get that. How's that working out for you?"

Sophie hadn't given a hoot about his age, hadn't ever felt the difference in their ages. Until recently. "It hasn't been a problem."

"I'm not surprised about that," Annie said. "You aren't one to get caught up in the status quo. You've lived your whole life outside the stereotypical box. So, do you two ever struggle to find things to talk about? Or to find common ground in how you feel about issues?"

"Never." If anything, the opposite was true. They seemed to view the world as one. They often talked long into the night, leaving them both struggling to get through work the next day. They talked about life and the world. About society and family. And faith. About anything except their other relationships.

Duane had never even heard of Annie.

"How do you feel when you're with him?"

Sophie pictured Duane sitting on the edge of her bed, putting on his shoes. "Comfortable," she said. Then, seeing him at her front door, smiling as he said hello, she added, "And energized at the same time. It's weird, really. It's like excited peace. If that makes any sense."

"It sounds like love to me." Annie pushed her glass aside. "Sophie, you know more than most that sometimes life creates its own definitions," she said, her voice intense.

"Not too many girls celebrate each birthday with a different father."

Stepfather, Sophie clarified silently. And it hadn't been every year—sometimes the divorces took longer than expected. Still, it had been often enough.

Duane didn't know about that, either.

"Nor do they have to be savvy enough to ward off advances from the father in residence by the time they're thirteen."

Though she shuddered, Sophie couldn't let herself dwell on the past. She'd forgiven her mother for her weaknesses a long time ago. And moved on.

Now her father—the real one, the man who'd left before she'd even been old enough to remember him—was another story. Forgiving him was harder. Only a jerk would abandon an innocent child to a whore.

Or maybe it was easier for her to blame a nameless, faceless entity.

"In some ways, you were raising a child—yourself—when *you* were a child," Annie continued more softly. "Which puts your maturity on more of an equal level with Duane than your ages would imply."

She was right. In some ways.

"But you knew all this, didn't you? Or you wouldn't have gotten involved with him to begin with."

Sophie nodded. "Our age difference is only one of many things that are wrong."

Eyes narrowed, Annie sat back. "He's not married, is he?"

"No." Though Sophie couldn't blame Annie for asking. "He was divorced years ago. Long before I met him."

"Any kids who hate you because you're closer to their age than his?"

"Nope. No kids."

"He's not an alcoholic, is he? Or abusive?"

"Of course not. Duane's the most upstanding citizen I've ever met. And that's a big part of the problem."

"Because he's a great guy?"

"He's too good for me."

"Bullsh—crap." Red blotches stood out on Annie's scrubbed cheeks.

"Or, rather, I'm not good enough for him."

"Stop it. Right now. What's gotten into you, girl? This isn't the Sophie I know. The one who had the courage to look life straight in the eye, take it on and win. There isn't a man alive who's too good for you."

Two years ago, while she'd still been celibate, Sophie would have agreed. Eight years ago, she'd have known the words for the lie they'd have been.

"Maybe not, if he were just a man. Trouble is, Duane's so much more than that." And before Annie could interject with another diatribe assuring Sophie that no man was more than any other—a reassurance she would love to hear, but that would net nothing—she continued, "He's running for public office, Annie. For the state senate. He's got so much energy. So many ideas. He's smart and savvy, openminded without being easily led. And most important, he's honest. Arizona—this country—needs him. And he's a shoo-in to win."

She'd never met any of his friends. Didn't know many of their names. She'd never been to the condominium he owned. Or to his law office.

But she knew about his politics.

"And you think you're somehow going to hurt his chances?"

"I know I would."

"How so? Because of the age difference?"

"That's part of it. How responsible is he going to look, at forty-six, squiring around a twentysomething blonde? One who's involved in the theater, no less? It's the typical midlife crisis. If nothing else, he'd lose the votes of all the middle-aged women who've lost their husbands to younger wives."

"But then, if you're going on that theory, he might gain votes from all of the men who understand, right?"

"Only those whose vote he'd have had anyway," Sophie said, having stayed up far too many nights in the past weeks researching twenty years of Arizona voting demographics in an attempt to calm fears she'd only exacerbated. "Men aren't as likely to cast their vote based on emotions, or personal circumstances."

"There are plenty of older politicians whose younger wives haven't kept them from office. There have even been some from Arizona."

"My age isn't everything," Sophie said, sinking into the helplessness that had been sapping so much of her mental energy these days. "My reputation leaves a lot to be desired, as well." There were other things, but this one Annie knew about. She'd been there.

"You were a college kid, Soph. Lots of coeds get a little wild for a year or two."

"Not as wild as I did. And most of them stick to guys their own age. Who aren't married."

"You were looking for security. To be cared for. Protected."

"I was acting like my mother's child."

"But at the same time, you won a scholarship to one of the nation's most prestigious universities, from which you graduated with honors. And in a few short years, you've made a name for yourself in an industry that is almost predominantly male. Your net worth has got to be more than most middle-class couples when they retire."

Sophie didn't discuss her income with anyone—including Duane. But Annie was in the business. She knew what kind of money was involved in production. And she knew how many shows Sophie did.

What she didn't know was that a good portion of Sophie's income went to organizations that provided older, sibling-type companions to troubled or lonely kids. And provided after-school facilities to them, as well.

"Have you and Duane talked about any of this?" Annie asked, after too long a silence.

"Some." The age difference. Her past reputation, which he'd have learned from his friend Will Parsons. And the politics.

"And?"

"He asked me to marry him."

CHAPTER THREE

"He asked you to marry him?" Annie squealed, but not so loudly that other patrons looked over at them, thank goodness. "See, he's not worried at all."

Sophie didn't share her friend's excitement. "He's asked before."

"How many times?"

"I don't know. Maybe six. Or seven. He knows I'm going to say no."

But he didn't know her middle name. And she hadn't asked his.

She hadn't asked to see his condo, either.

Duane had his place in her life. Nice. Neat. Clean. Controlled.

"And?" Annie asked again, as their waitress refilled their glasses of tea.

"He's always relieved when I do."

"He is? You sure about that?"

"Of course. I'm not alone in my fears, Annie. Duane feels them, too. Why do you think we've been seeing each other for two years and you're only now hearing about him? Other than Will Parsons, he hasn't told any of his friends, either. And he wouldn't have told Will except that we see each other in Shelter Valley, which meant Will was going to hear about it anyway."

"He's been keeping you a secret?" Annie's words held accusation.

"We decided together to keep quiet about our friendship." No one would understand. But their choices suited them. Until they didn't.

"Do Matt and Phyllis know?"

Like Sophie, Annie had taken several classes with Matt Sheffield—the Montford Performing Arts Center director and instructor who Sophie had once tried to sleep with. Annie knew his wife, Phyllis, too.

"Of course."

Phyllis, a psychology professor at Montford, had been largely responsible for Sophie's chance at a healthy life. While Sophie had been busy convincing herself that Matt was in love with her, Phyllis had been diagnosing Sophie's bulimia.

"So you're still seeing them as much?"

"Mmm-hmm. We go back and forth with each other almost every day when I'm home. I can't seem to go much longer than that without seeing the twins."

"You've been here two weeks and haven't even mentioned Calvin and Clarissa. How are they?"

"Good," she said, wondering how soon she could excuse herself and go back to her hotel room. She had some serious business to attend to. A head to get under control. Immediately.

And maybe a decision to make? Was her relationship with Duane coming to an end? They'd both known it would have to happen eventually.

Hadn't they?

"They're six and a half now, can you believe that?" Sophie said, to continue the innocuous conversation.

"No way!" Annie's surprise mirrored Sophie's own. Even seeing the kids so often, it was hard to believe how quickly they were growing up. How quickly life passed. Phyllis had just found out she was pregnant when Sophie had first met her.

Sophie grabbed her digital camera from her purse, clicked in view mode and scrolled through the photos. "Here," she said, handing the camera to her friend. "That was taken Christmas afternoon." Only a few weeks ago. The kids, with Sophie in between them, were standing in front of their Christmas tree.

"Clarissa's a looker already, with those big brown eyes and that long hair."

"Yeah, she turns heads everywhere she goes. A real princess, but you wouldn't know it by talking to her," Sophie said, not that she was proud of the kids or anything. "Phyllis has them both in karate."

"I'm not surprised after everything Calvin went through." The boy had been abducted when he was two—by another ex-student of Matt's. "What happened to that girl? Shelly was her name, right?"

"Yeah, Shelly Monroe." Sophie had never met the girl, but had a love-hate relationship with her. In some ways, she'd been a clone of the girl—clinging to Matt for security in the aftermath of an abusive childhood. But thankfully, that was where their resemblance ended. "She's in prison, doing twenty years for an assortment of charges. I missed the day of sentencing so I'm not sure what she was convicted of."

"Her twelve-year-old son had been killed in a gang shooting, right?"

"Apparently, she was living in a pretty rough area and

somehow blamed Matt for all of her unhappiness because he hadn't saved her from herself. She figured he owed her, and took Matt's son to replace the one she lost."

There'd been a car wreck as she'd fled. But other than bruises and a broken arm, Calvin had been okay.

"What about Phyllis's newfound twin sister—Caroline, wasn't it? Is she still around?"

"Oh yeah, she and John were over for Christmas dinner along with their three-year-old daughter, Sara, and Caroline's son, Jesse. He's twenty and just graduated from Harvard." When Sophie had told Duane about him later that evening, during their own private holiday celebration at her house, he'd asked too many questions, stopped just short of making an accusation that would have changed the tenor of their relationship. Hard to imagine he'd been jealous of a twenty-year-old kid.

Sophie didn't want to think about that right now. "Caroline's this really shy woman from Kentucky, and I thought she was going to melt to the floor when she heard her three-year-old ask for more presents."

"Kind of like the girl I knew who wanted to sink beneath a front porch one Christmas day after the older man she'd just publicly confessed her love to confessed his love to their pregnant hostess?"

Annie was referring to Sophie and Matt and Phyllis Sheffield before they'd been married. Almost eight years ago. The worst—and best—day of Sophie's life.

They caught her throwing up the Christmas dinner Phyllis had prepared and Sophie had consumed in humongous quantities.

"Until tonight I hadn't thrown up once since then," she said now, softly.

"And you've been friends with Duane for two years," Annie said. "So why now?"

Sophie wasn't sure. Or didn't want to be. But she had learned a lot of painful lessons on her road to recovery. The first and foremost being you didn't hide from anything. Didn't push anything away. Because issues, problems, really didn't go. They stayed buried inside you where they could attack from the inside out.

"Duane's said a few things… I don't know. I just get the idea he's worried that if there are hard times, I'll revert to the…woman I was."

"What? A bulimic? He might get bronchitis someday, too. So you treat the illness and move on. I don't—"

"It's not about the bulimia," Sophie interrupted. "Or, at least, not really. I think he's afraid that I'm emotionally weak, and sees the bulimia as evidence of that. But that's not the part that bothers him. He knows that I'm responsible and would get help if it ever arose again."

But would he really stand by her? What would Duane say if she called him right now? Told him what had happened tonight? Would he still be at her house tomorrow? As he'd promised during their last intimate call?

"Then what—"

"I think he's afraid that deep down I get my confidence and self-worth from men. That he can't trust me to be faithful to him."

"What makes you think that?"

"He gets really quiet sometimes. Usually when I've mentioned talking to some other man. Then I don't hear from him for a day or two."

"Do you ask him about it?"

"Of course. He always says nothing was wrong, and he's

got an excuse as to why he didn't call. They're usually good excuses."

"You were never once unfaithful in a relationship."

"I was never in any real relationships." Duane was the first. Hard to believe from a woman with her experience. "And, considering how many lovers I've had, how can I expect him to see me as anything but a woman who needs multiple men?"

"You haven't had a lover, other than Duane, since Matt and Phyllis helped you acknowledge the bulimia, have you?" Annie asked.

"No."

"Does Duane know that?"

"I told him."

"And?"

"He says he believes me. He says my past is past."

"But you don't believe he means it."

Sophie shrugged. "I wouldn't blame him if he doubted me."

Annie watched her. "Is that because you doubt yourself?"

"I know I can be faithful to him."

"Of course you can. You know your worth now, Soph. You know that it's not found in some man's arms. Or in any man's opinion of you."

She'd thought so—until the fear of losing Duane had started to take hold of her. She'd seen the writing on the wall—several times—over the past months as Duane's political backers became more obvious in their intentions to name him as their candidate in the upcoming election.

People would want to know about the man who sought the power to pass laws in their state. The press would start to dig.

Her and Duane's safe little world would be exposed. Her past would be exposed.

And she'd lose him. Would be completely alone again.

And she'd started to be more concerned about how she looked. Needing to be certain, if she was going to be single again, that she was still attractive.

She didn't feel attractive.

"So why do I suddenly feel so unworthy? So…ugly?" she asked, a question reminiscent of the olden days. Certainly the Sophie she'd become would never have allowed herself to be so vulnerable.

Another sign of the depths to which she'd sunk?

Annie's gaze grew shadowed and she leaned forward. "It has nothing to do with the way you look. You couldn't be ugly if you tried, Soph. You're one of the most beautiful women I've ever known. You always have been. Those long legs and flat stomach are the envy of every dancer on your stages. And your features are classically perfect."

She liked her nose. The rest was too…this. Too that.

"You have all those things going for you, but it's never enough," Annie continued. "You seem to think you have to be physically perfect to be good enough, and that's a lost cause. No one is perfect. We're all flawed. And we're all beautiful, too.

"What matters is what's inside the package," Annie said, her eyes softening. "You know that. And you're beautiful there, Soph. Even more than on the outside. You keep to yourself too much these days, but the you that's in there still comes out through your work. You know precisely what lights to use, precisely what shadowing or backdrop, what depth, what timing, what colors to make everything onstage look like more than it is. You take the art we work so hard to perform and make it magic."

"I went to school to learn how to do that."

"So did a million other people and no one does a show like you do. Even you can't argue with the amazing success of Sophie Productions. Your shows have heart, depth. They speak to every single sense every single minute, engaging the audience's full attention. Performers, directors want you for a reason, Soph, and it's not your great bod."

"What about Sam Wynn?" Sophie interjected, needing to distance herself a little bit from Annie's intensity. An intensity that matched the emotions churning inside her.

"He's a jerk and should be arrested for the way he came on to you."

Sam wasn't the only one. He'd happened to be working on a show Annie was in, so her friend knew about that one.

Mostly the advances, the come-ons, didn't matter to Sophie. She'd learned to take them in stride, to blow them off, years ago. Mostly.

A guy she'd once slept with told her she "exuded." She couldn't remember the guy's name. Couldn't really even remember what he looked like. But she remembered those words.

"Exuded what?" she'd asked.

He hadn't been able to tell her.

She'd watched herself over the years, pulled inside herself more and more in an attempt to make sure she didn't keep doing whatever it was she did. But it seemed to happen anyway.

And so she'd made certain that no one got too close. No one saw all of her.

Duane came closest. Sort of.

And he knew she exuded. He saw whatever it was she missed. He reacted to it.

Not that he'd said so.

But Sophie knew.

Was it also what drew him to her?

Was he, in his own sweet way, just like all the rest?

Sophie didn't know, but she had a feeling that whatever it was she did around men was something she'd been doing since birth. Inadvertently inviting them, tempting them, to hurt her.

CHAPTER FOUR

DUANE GLANCED AT HIS ROLEX, a gift from the other partners in his firm a couple of Christmases ago. Six-fifteen.

The table was set. With her regular dishes and silver, the ones he'd used with her many times in the past. She had china and table linens—he'd been treated to a couple of anniversary celebrations on them—but Duane felt uncomfortable enough about being in Sophie's place without her. He couldn't bring himself to look through drawers and cupboards that she hadn't specifically invited him into.

He'd had the key to her place for over a year—to let himself out those days he had to leave before dawn to get to court in Phoenix, and hadn't wanted her to have to drag herself out of bed to lock the dead bolt after him. But he'd never been in her small home without her before.

She'd invited him to use the place like his own. To stay there, if he wanted to get out of the city, when she was out of town.

He hadn't.

After another peek at his watch, he checked the foil-wrapped potatoes he'd put in the oven almost an hour before. They were softening nicely.

A glance in the refrigerator assured him that the steaks had stayed right where he'd left them, soaking in his own special marinade recipe in the Ziploc bag on the second shelf. And the salad still looked crisp.

Six-twenty. The table might not look like much—certainly nothing resembling the lavish, something-from-a-magazine settings Sophie had made for them over the past couple of years—but the flowers were noticeable. He'd personally chosen every single bloom—going heavy on the red roses. Chosen the delicately colored, handwoven basket they were in, as well.

And waited at a specialty importer in Phoenix, one of few florists open on Sunday, while they were arranged.

He might be a man—a lawyer and not talented in the ways of his artistically creative lover—but he could still manage to pull together something special.

For Sophie.

Something in the woman made him capable of moving mountains.

For her.

Six-thirty.

Her flight had been scheduled to land in Phoenix at five. If luggage had arrived in a timely fashion, she could be driving up any minute.

And somehow he had to pull this off. This dinner. This life. He wasn't ready. It didn't take a genius to figure that out. But time wasn't waiting for him. He might not have what it took to be there for Sophie in the long run, might not have the confidence to squire a young beauty around town and not get jealous when other men paid attention to her. He might not be man enough to keep her interest, her faithfulness, in the years to come, but if he didn't try, he wasn't going to have Sophie.

Patting his jacket, feeling for the thickness of the card

he'd slipped into the inside pocket, Duane paced for the umpteenth time from the dining area into the living room and back. Straightened the knot in his tie. Now wasn't the time to ponder things that were out of his control. Things that were probably not worth pondering.

Now was not the time to get himself worked up over what could go wrong.

Now was the time to think about what was.

Sophie Curtis was a nationally acclaimed theatrical producer who'd put herself through college, owned her home and had true friends who stood by her.

She was also the only woman who'd ever been able, or cared enough, to scale his walls and find his heart.

Six-forty. One more glance out the window on his way through the living room.

"This is ridiculous." His voice, sounding so loud in the silence, startled him.

And reminded him that he needed some tunes. Mood music. Turning on the stereo occupied about ten seconds. He went for the light-rock station that he and Sophie preferred.

Though he'd tried a time or two, he'd not been able to entice her over to his jazz station. She and Jean Luc Ponty had yet to bond.

And if they never did, that was fine. Lots of couples—longtime married, happy couples—had different tastes in music.

Duane slid a hand into his pants pocket, seeking and finding its sole occupant—the ring he'd purchased a week ago, and picked up that afternoon. Turned out jewelers in Phoenix were open even on Sundays. The velvet-lined case, a dead giveaway, was out in his car.

He wanted to surprise her.

Life presented a lot of unanswered questions, but, finding himself at a crossroads that was going to make decisions for him if he waited too long, Duane had done some heavy thinking.

And come up with one sure thing.

He wasn't ready to tell Sophie Curtis goodbye.

Six forty-five. Noticing the path he was wearing in her freshly vacuumed cream-colored carpet, he sank into the leather chair in front of the fireplace. When she was home, they sat on the love seat.

Unless they were lying in front of the television. Then they used the sofa.

Raising his ankle to his knee, Duane studied the shine on his wingtip shoe. As far as he could tell the day had produced only one smudge.

He tried to care, but couldn't work up the focus. Where was Sophie?

Would she be as glad to see him as he would be to see her?

Had she missed him as much?

Would she accept the ring?

And was that someone at the front door? Was she looking for her key? Had she lost it in the bottom of her bag? Why hadn't he heard her car? And why hadn't she pulled into the garage and come in through the kitchen like she usually did?

Like he'd planned?

He'd wanted her to see the flowers first.

With nerves tensing his stomach, Duane strode to the front door, a smile of welcome on his lips—in his heart—and a full-carat solitaire diamond burning against his leg.

"Welcome ho—" His voice broke off as he saw the inexpensively dressed, fiftysomething man standing there with a warm smile spread across his face.

"Oh, sorry." The man straightened, and Duane noticed the brown paper bag he'd just left next to the decorative stone beside Sophie's front door. The stranger seemed surprised to see Duane there.

The feeling was mutual.

"I, um, left some welcome-home cookies. Chocolate chip."

Sophie's favorite. And how did this man know that?

For that matter, how did he know Sophie at all?

Intending to grill the stranger as though he were on trial, Duane affected the proper, intimidating pose, and intended to deliver his first put-the-witness-firmly-in-his-place question.

"You from around here?" he asked when his brain let him down.

"For now."

What in the hell did that mean? He waited for the older man to expound. And wasn't sure what to do when, instead, the man turned and walked to an older blue pickup parked opposite the house, climbed in, gunned the engine and drove off.

Without another glance at Duane.

As though Duane didn't matter at all.

SHE'D MEANT TO DRIVE slowly, to use the hour between Phoenix and Shelter Valley as a calming time, a reconnection with personal peace and the self she'd come to know and love over the past eight years.

Instead of keeping her mind on the things she'd intended, all she could think about was getting home by seven. To be there when Duane arrived.

To feel his arms around her.

It had been a long two weeks.

Too long.

She'd missed him horribly.

And knew their days were numbered.

They couldn't keep pretending that what they had was working.

Dressed in one of her nicer pairs of jeans, black suede boots and a black sweater that was a favorite of Duane's, Sophie pushed her Ford Explorer Sport Trac as much past the speed limit as she dared without risking a ticket. She thought about stopping for Chinese takeout rather than going to a restaurant near Tucson as they'd planned. She didn't want to share him with waitresses and other patrons tonight.

In isolation they were perfect together.

And reality was intruding. Making her ill.

Because reality was not a part of life she could avoid, because she knew her fantasy life with Duane had come to an end, Sophie drove straight home, watching for his car as she pulled off the highway, through town and toward the secluded street of custom homes not far from Matt and Phyllis's place. Hers was the smallest house on the block, but it was all hers. She'd contracted it, chosen the floor plan and every single color and fixture inside. She'd spent evenings and weekends on-site, checking the progress, and even some days, watching the men work.

And right now, with Duane's silver Mercedes parked out front, the small, stuccoed structure with its vibrantly colored landscaping had never looked better.

Even with things falling apart around them, she was glad he was here.

It was better to see him than to not see him. For the moment.

Sophie waited while the garage door rose, then pulled in. She'd never had anyone to come home to before. Never had anyone waiting.

"And don't make too much of it, girl," she mumbled aloud as she grabbed her purse and climbed out. Her luggage could wait.

Duane's presence was a one-time thing—an occasional thing at most. She lived alone.

And when one lived alone, one came home to an empty house.

That's just the way it was.

The way she wanted it to be. Most of the time. The way she needed it to be. Anything else made life messy.

And messy made her sick.

But that didn't mean she had to ruin this moment, she reminded herself as she opened the door into the house.

Something smelled wonderful.

And not at all like the Chinese dinner she'd envisioned picking up on the way home.

The door hadn't fully closed behind her before Duane appeared at the end of the hall, holding two glasses of champagne.

"Welcome home, babe."

With knees gone uncharacteristically weak, Sophie managed the two steps to reach him, steadying herself, and him, with her hands atop his on the glasses, and leaned forward to kiss him.

Long.

And again.

Her mouth opened, her tongue met his, and she didn't want to let go, to break away and face reality.

Time, society, ages, past mistakes and bulimia all faded away when Duane's tongue was in her mouth.

"I missed you," she said, finally pulling back far enough to reconnect with those deep chocolate eyes that could look at her with such warmth.

They weren't letting her in. Not completely.

But then, it had been two weeks. And times were hard. Their struggles were not a secret.

"Here." Duane held out her glass, the smile on his lips completely genuine. "Here's to you coming home to me." The softness in his voice made up for the slight distance in his gaze.

Their glasses clinked. Looking at each other, they sipped.

"Mmm, this is the good stuff."

"Only the best for this…for you."

Duane turned away, saying something about steaks as he set his glass on the counter and rummaged in the refrigerator. Chattering about marinade, he made his way out to the grill on the back patio.

Something was underfoot. The champagne. An apparently very nice dinner prepared. The beautiful rose-filled centerpiece on the table. And…her companion. The completely self-assured, argue-with-God-in-court-and-win Duane Koch was nervous.

And that made her nervous.

Sophie's stomach clenched and there was no time for happy thoughts. For prevention. She barely made it to the bathroom before the champagne came back up on her.

LUCKILY, IT DIDN'T TAKE Sophie as long to tend to her illness as it did Duane to cook steaks. With too many years of practice she'd largely learned to hide her little forays into the darkness. Only Phyllis, Matt and Annie had ever caught her in the act.

And, on the side of preserving a moment, once she'd regurgitated, she always had an appetite.

Sitting with Duane at her kitchen table, her senses consumed with him, Sophie ate, took a few more sips of champagne. Laughed in the right places. Shared the highlights of this latest performance with him. Told him about meeting up with an old college friend—taking great care to stress that the friend was female.

And she caught up on the past two weeks of Duane's life.

He'd won his party's nomination for the senate seat.

Now she understood the celebration. And, most likely, the distance in his eyes, as well.

Her place in his life and his bid for office did not coincide. And the dichotomy was a symbol of all the other struggles their differences created. The ticking of their clock was growing louder.

So, tonight, this celebration was for Duane.

Tomorrow she was going straight to Phyllis.

The counselor, not the friend.

CHAPTER FIVE

THERE WERE SO MANY THINGS Duane had to say. And none of them were getting out beyond the inane, superficial conversation he and Sophie had fallen into—largely, he suspected, caused by him.

He reached for his napkin, and his knuckles scraped against that thin piece of metal resting against his thigh, and he took another sip of champagne.

The box was in the car because he'd wanted to surprise her, wasn't it?

And not so that he could change his mind without her being any the wiser?

"My friend, the one I saw in Chicago, has a show in Phoenix later this spring at the Orpheum. I want you to meet her."

Sophie's sweet green eyes met his, an unusual pleading in their depths that had absolutely nothing to do with her friend, and Duane's appetite receded.

"I'd like that," he said. "Very much." Sophie was an incredible woman. He wanted to know everything about her. Wanted to know everyone she knew, to have a chance to care about everyone she cared about. Yet his life had nothing in common with hers.

Her hand, so slim and delicate considering the ropes she

wielded, the heavy travelers she pulled open and closed, the scrims and cycs she lowered, rested on the table next to her plate. Duane laid his palm over it.

"I… We need to talk," he started, then issued a silent curse when he heard the ominous way that had come out— as though he had bad news. "I mean—"

"It's okay." Her smile was more sad than anything. She shifted her hand and reversed their positions. "I'll make this easy for you."

She knew? How could she have guessed? He hadn't known himself, for sure, until today, when he'd actually picked up the ring. And he still wasn't sure. How could she possibly make this easy?

"No." He shook his head. "I'm going to get this right," he said, focusing on what he knew. On the man he knew himself to be. Once he committed to doing something, he was in one hundred percent.

Get down, man. On your knee. You know the drill.

"I love you." That seemed to say everything he was trying to get out.

Which didn't explain the moisture in Sophie's eyes. She wasn't a crier.

"And I love you," she said. "But that's not going to be enough, is it?" Her whispered words were lost on him at first, caught up as he was in the haze of panic the moment wrought.

He wasn't ready to lose her. But as much as he loved being here with her, he wasn't sure he wanted her in Phoenix, too. Wasn't sure he could trust himself to risk the life he'd built there.

He was forty-six years old. Reaching goals he'd spent his entire life seeking. Forty-six, not twenty-six. He didn't have a lifetime stretching ahead to make something of himself.

Those years were streaming behind him. A path to where he was now. To what he might have to give up.

But that's not going to be enough, is it? Her words finally reached him.

"What does that mean? It's not enough?"

"We can be in love all we want, but love can't change the facts. When we're here, alone, you don't have to worry about other men looking at me. About me talking with other men. And I don't have to worry about how I appear to the people who matter in your life. Love isn't going to make you look any less like those fifty-year-old guys who drive convertibles with the tops down in forty-degree weather when you're with me. You'd lose credibility."

Duane didn't want to hear her.

"No one said it's going to be easy," he told her, "or that there wouldn't be problems."

He waited for her to help him out—mostly because he had no idea what to do here. She sat watching him, apparently waiting for more.

He wanted—needed—to give her more. But his mind seemed to be frozen. He'd come to propose. He had unresolved issues with proposing.

He cared about her a great deal.

"I know us being together won't be easy." He had to say something. They were both waiting on him. "But I can't walk away from you, Soph. That's it for me. My bottom line. I can't walk away."

Seconds passed. And then some more. God, he wished she'd say something. Anything. Give him some clue to what she was thinking behind that half frown and those tear-glazed eyes. But he made himself wait.

Made himself give her time.

Maybe the struggle wasn't worth it to her. She was young. Had her whole life ahead of her. Didn't need to settle for all the problems being with him brought her. Didn't—

"I…guess I'm not ready to walk away, either," she said.

Duane tried to tamp down the relief flooding through him. She was letting him off the hook. Again. But he had to be smart here. Responsible. Make sound decisions. "You don't seem too happy about that."

Sophie's shrug said so much. He only wished he could decipher what.

They were at a standstill. Staring at each other. Waiting for something to happen.

Duane dropped to one knee.

"Sophie Curtis, will you marry me?" The words came out exactly as he'd said them every other time he'd asked.

But he'd never had a ring in his pocket.

"Duane, get up." Sophie tugged on his hand. "You don't have to do this."

But their world was quickly crumbling. He had to do something.

"You're twenty-eight, Soph. You're going to be wanting kids. And if I don't start having them soon, I'm going to be too old to play with them. Or even make it to their graduation."

"You're forty-six," she said. "You've got a good forty years left in you. At least. I hardly think we have to worry about wheeling your chair to any graduation."

She was splitting hairs. And so was he.

But he couldn't stop the wheels from turning.

"Besides," she continued, while he tried to catch up with the situation, "I'm not ready to have kids yet. Not until I'm at the point where I can consult on shows, but not have to be on-site and produce them. For now, I travel way too much."

"So stop. Matt's the production manager at Montford, but there are other universities in the state. Or what about the Orpheum? Or Symphony Hall? Or Gammage? What about Herberger or the Celebrity Theater? Or even Cricket Pavilion? Instead of working for everyone, you could work full-time for one theater. Run your own show at home."

"It sounds as though you've considered my possibilities." The little smile tilting her lips snagged his heart.

"Of course I have." Duane leaned forward, grabbing both of her hands, that smile driving him in spite of his need to put on the brake. "I mean this, Sophie. I think we should get married." He paused. "If you want your future to be with me."

She was young and beautiful. What in the hell was he doing, thinking she'd want to tie herself to him permanently?

He'd lost his mind.

"Of course I want my future with you," she said, though she didn't sound any more sure than he felt. "You wouldn't have a key to my home, or have ever been invited back after that night we met, if I didn't want you in my life. Before you, I hadn't dated in almost five years, Duane. That was my choice. Not because I didn't want to marry and have a family, but because I wasn't going to screw up again. I knew that when I met the man I wanted for keeps, I'd know it."

His heart pounding, Duane still felt something settle within him. Something good.

Until he started thinking again. "And did you know it? When we first met?"

"No."

He tried not to let the disappointment crush him.

"I knew it the morning after, when I woke up with you and didn't hate myself for being in bed with you. Being with you felt so right."

No wonder he hadn't wanted to get out of bed that morning. And why something about her had been calling him back ever since.

"Then it's time to get married."

"If it were time to get married, you wouldn't be having such a hard time getting through this."

Oh, he loved this woman. Loved how well she knew him.

And was scared as hell by it, too.

"I'm having a hard time because I know how important it is that we do this. I know how much is resting on it."

"What's that mean?"

"I've agreed to run for state office. You're right. People are going to be watching me. Judging me. Looking for smut. I don't care so much for myself, but I care for you. If we don't get married, we'd have to quit seeing each other, because it's unlikely we'd be blessed with a miracle and be able to keep our liaison secret. You'd be found out and called my whore."

"Your midlife crisis."

"Right."

"Which would hurt your chances of getting elected."

"Yes." And that bothered him.

"But maybe we aren't ready for scrutiny yet." Sophie paused, frowning. "Or maybe there's more that needs to happen in our individual lives before we can settle into being a generational couple."

Could she mean she had more seeds to sow?

A vision he'd been blocking for the past couple of hours haunted Duane, sending shards of dread through him all over again.

A simple brown bag on her front porch.

"If I promise to understand that this time you mean your proposal, and that you're serious about us getting married soon, can we postpone this conversation for a day or two? Let me have some time to settle in and think?"

Relief had been understandable half an hour ago, when he'd found out she still cared. It wasn't so forgivable now—not when she was postponing something he should want more than anything else on earth.

"Of course." He relented before she could change her mind. "I've been thinking about this since you left," he told her. "I'm a bit ahead of you."

"You're always ahead of me," she said with a chuckle. "I've never met anyone as clear thinking as you are. That's one of the things I love so much about you—your ability to see through the muck to what's really there."

"To cut to the chase," he murmured, recognizing what she was telling him about himself. He'd been praised for the talent many times in his legal profession.

So why, when it came to Sophie, were his thoughts anything but clear?

Sophie slid to her knees, the heels of her boots visible behind her. "Counselor, could you please give me a recess, just until tomorrow morning so that we can go into the bedroom and have recess for real?"

He recognized what she was doing. Diverting them, returning them to the world where they were perfect—alone, just the two of them.

Their fantasy.

It was what they always did when reality intervened. Retreated.

But the fantasy wasn't working anymore.

Sophie's hand on his thigh was. He was already hard. Anticipating. When it came to sex, she never failed to arouse him. Not ever.

"Please take me to bed, babe." Sophie's voice took on a note of quiet desperation. "Hold me and make the world's craziness go away. Long enough for me to get some rest?"

"You haven't been sleeping well?" She hadn't said anything. And he'd called her every single night she'd been gone.

"Honestly?"

"Of course."

"I never sleep well when you aren't with me."

She did have a way with words. Or, more precisely, her words had a way with him.

"Another reason why we should get married," he said, even when he knew he didn't want to push the point.

"I know."

But she still didn't say yes. And he wasn't any more sure he was ready for her to do so.

For tonight he needed to feel her skin against his, to lose himself in her scent, in her arms, in her center, and visit once again the heaven that had been created for the two of them.

Fifteen minutes later, after cleaning up, retrieving her luggage and turning off the lights, Duane walked hand in hand with Sophie down the hall to the master suite, thinking only of getting her warm body as close to his as he could.

CHAPTER SIX

WIDE-AWAKE, Sophie stared at the ceiling—or what she could see of it in the moonlight. Her body was completely sated, satisfied, loved. She'd been consumed by Duane's lovemaking like never before. In tune with his every touch, she'd felt precious, powerful, the most beautiful woman in the world.

Then, with their hips pressed up against each other, they'd drifted off to sleep.

Problem was, she'd woken up. And with Duane's head resting on her shoulder, his hand still covering her breast, she didn't want to move and disturb him. She wanted him right where he was—needed him there. Where no one could see them. Disturb them.

Challenge them.

In bed with Duane, alone with him, she knew she'd never have to sabotage herself again. Never have to sub-consciously prove her inner strength through carefully mastering of base appetites. She'd never have to fight feelings of emotional scarcity.

But she couldn't live her life in bed with Duane.

Tomorrow would come—as it always did. To shine light on things that went unnoticed in the darkness.

And while Duane was always an incredible lover, part

of him had been more distant tonight. He was pulling away from her.

She knew that. Understood it.

And maybe he was withholding from himself, as well. Pushing himself into something he wasn't sure was right.

If he'd really wanted to marry her, they'd be married by now.

Wouldn't they?

She listened to Duane's even breathing. Counted the beats of his heart against her side.

Every instinct she had told her that for them to marry under pressure—because, with his nomination, they either had to marry or split—would be a recipe for disaster.

She couldn't afford another personal disaster. You could only bankrupt your heart so many times before it gave out on you. Or gave up on you.

"What are you thinking about?" His voice was strong, steady. Not sleepy at all.

He hadn't moved. And neither did she.

"How long have you been awake?"

"Most of the night."

The fact that he wasn't resting any easier than she was scared her. Duane was usually out as soon as he lay down. And slept all night. He kept a schedule that would challenge a man half his age. He needed his rest.

He'd asked what she was thinking about. If she brought up the problems between them, would she lose him?

Was she ready to do that?

No. She wanted to bury her head in the sand. Be on vacation. Pretend. Live for the moment.

She couldn't run from her doubts. They'd only catch up with her. They always did. At far too high a price.

Running her fingers through his hair, she said, "I've been lying here trying to figure out what's different about you tonight."

"Different how?"

"I'm not sure. It feels like you're holding back. And yet I can't give you any evidence to support the feeling."

The hand on her breast slid away. "Feelings are the one fallacy of the factual system," he said, rolling over until his head rested on the pillow right beside hers, touching hers. "So much of the time, they don't make sense."

"So I'm right. You're holding back."

"No. I don't think so. At all." The protest, though a little too forced, was at least something to clutch on to.

Her stomach, which had been working its way into a small frenzy, relaxed a bit.

"But I'm sensing something?"

"Nothing more than the confusion of having what I want be at odds with what I need."

She didn't ask which she was—the want or the need. Or if she was even what he was talking about.

A year ago, she would have been positive she knew both—his wants and needs. A year ago, when there'd been no visible cracks in their idyllic hideaway life, his wants and needs hadn't been a threat.

"We shouldn't have to work so hard to make this work."

"Relationships, even the best of them, are hard work. Always."

"You sound awfully certain about that for a man who's lived alone most of his life."

"I had the very best teacher."

"Who?" She had no idea because, outside of her home, she knew very little about him.

"Will Parsons."

"What does Will have to do with us?"

"You weren't in Shelter Valley yet when Becca got pregnant, were you?"

"No." But she'd come to know the couple well enough through Matt and Phyllis, and had been accepted into their peripheral family circle, in spite of her past.

"Anybody ever tell you their story?"

"I know the basics—high school sweethearts who married and weren't blessed with children until Becca was in her forties."

"That's the public version."

"It's not true?"

"Of course it is. Every bit of it. But there's more."

There always was, wasn't there? But what could there possibly be in that story that would emulate her with Duane? Becca and Will were obviously meant for each other. And everyone, including them, had known that from the time they were still practically kids.

"Becca was less than six months pregnant when Will came to me, discreetly, asking about divorce. Specifically, he'd wanted to know how he could end his marriage with Becca but still provide for her as though they were married—insurance, security, beneficiary of his will, that sort of thing."

Sophie sat up. Cold to the bone. "Will wanted to divorce Becca?"

Was nothing sacred?

"Under the circumstances, I don't think Will would mind my telling you. When Becca first found out she was pregnant, the prognosis was pretty scary to her. An over-forty pregnancy brought more risk of birth defects, and she'd already had several miscarriages. She had high blood pressure, plus she and Will had their careers, their busy schedules. The first doctor she went to recommended that she terminate the pregnancy."

"I can see why."

"So could Becca. She considered having it done."

"And?"

"Will couldn't understand. They'd waited their whole lives for this chance. He'd spent years comforting her, pulling her through depression when she'd lose another baby, spending huge amounts of money on tests and fertilization efforts and now, when they were given a miracle, Becca wanted to throw it away."

"Hardly that."

"I know." Duane turned his head on the pillow. Looked at her. "And eventually Will got it, too. But for a while there, he really struggled. He felt like he didn't know Becca at all. This woman whom he'd always considered the other half of his mind and soul suddenly took on characteristics he didn't understand. Then he started to question himself for questioning her. Did he love her, or was it only the image they'd built of the high school sweethearts meant for each other—an image that Shelter Valley had helped them build? That he clung to?"

"Wow." Picturing Will, Sophie could hardly believe what she was hearing. He was Godlike to his students. Always in control. Always had all the answers. Always made the right choices.

"They actually separated for a while."

She felt like a kid discovering that her parents had sex. Or at least, what she imagined that would feel like for most kids.

"Things were rough for a while, but, in the end, their

relationship is far stronger than it ever was. I've never seen two people more devoted and dedicated to each other."

Now that sounded like the Parsonses she knew.

"And the point is that relationships are hard work," Duane said, pushing himself up to lean against the headboard. "Even the ones that have everything going for them and should be easy."

Sophie sat up next to him, crossing her arms over her naked breasts.

"I'm not afraid of the work," she said. "Nothing in my life's been easy—except maybe knowing what lighting works onstage. But the kind of things we're facing aren't things we can change with effort. They're feelings and instincts and facts."

"Such as?"

"You're nervous about tying your life to me." He hadn't said so. But he hadn't had to. "And not in the way that guys get nervous when they're contemplating marriage. Or, if you are, then that's in addition to what I'm talking about. You're nervous about me. Specifically. In ways you wouldn't be if you were in love with a woman of your social class and age bracket."

Duane was still, his gaze seemingly focused straight ahead.

After an excruciating minute she asked, "Aren't you?"

"Maybe."

Sophie tried not to be crushed. Tried not to cry—all the while fighting the familiar feeling of not being good enough. Not being worthy. "What we're contemplating here is going to change our lives irrevocably, one way or the other, Duane," she said. "Whether we end up together or not. Let's at least be completely honest. We've got no hope at all if we can't be straight with each other."

She *was* good enough. She *was* worthy. She didn't used to believe that, but she did now.

Didn't she?

The insecurities were old habits.

Nothing more.

Several years ago when Phyllis had still been her counselor, she'd warned Sophie that old habits often resurfaced.

Sophie's thoughts chased themselves, her stomach rumbled and she waited for Duane to respond.

Waited to take whatever painful thing he had to say, to weather it and move on.

"Okay." He finally broke the silence and turned toward her. "I do worry."

Feeling like a masochist, she asked, "About what, specifically?"

"Aside from the fact that when I'm fifty-seven and you're thirty-nine, you're going to get turned off by my old man's body and start yearning for someone younger?"

Had she been of a different nature, Sophie might have slapped his face for that one.

Instead she jutted her chin to stop it from trembling, and tried to accept the facts. Whether she liked them or not.

"So, you're saying that I'm interested in you, attracted to you, because of your physical attributes."

"Of course. It's natural. Physical attraction is as old as the world."

"And you think your forty-six-year-old body is as sexy as, say, the thirty-year-old dancer I watched onstage for the past two weeks?"

Maybe she was being cruel. Maybe even deliberately, a little bit. He'd hurt her.

She wasn't a whore who jumped from bed to bed. Who jumped for the male body, period.

Maybe she had been. Once. But Duane hadn't known that woman. He'd only known this one.

"Is this your way of telling me you've spent the past two weeks lusting over some other guy's body? That when you had sex with me tonight you were thinking about him?"

He thought that poorly of her? That she'd do that? Pain seared through her, taking her to the darkness that had consumed her in her youth.

He's showing you his insecurities, her rational mind asserted.

She wanted Duane to accept her with all of her issues. Didn't that gift come with the obligation to do the same for him? To accept all of him, if she was going to commit to any of him?

Sophie took a deep breath. "No, Duane, I'm not telling you that at all. I didn't feel the slightest twinge for the guy. Couldn't even, after two weeks of setting lights on him, tell you his name. What I'm telling you is that it isn't your body that attracts me to you. The fact that it's gorgeous is a benefit, but I don't get turned on because you have a nice ass."

His eyes narrowed, but he said nothing.

"I get turned on by you. By the way your hands hold the wrench when you tighten the connection under the kitchen sink. By the way you respond with a sigh and collective commiseration for everyone involved when you're stuck in traffic. Or when someone knocks into you in the grocery store and you tell them they're all right. I get turned on by your laugh, how it bursts out when something really amuses you. And I like that what makes you laugh most is tongue-in-cheek humor. I get turned on by your thoughts and theories, and not only by how quickly you think, but also by how your mind wanders off on its own tracks. You don't automatically buy into what the world is saying, or accept the answers the world accepts. I get turned on by how you look at me…."

Sophie's words drifted off. She was making it harder for him to walk away. And if he couldn't stay without convincing, she didn't want him here.

But then, in spite of admonitions to herself, she added, "All of those things will still be there when you're eighty."

"You're telling me you're in love with me."

Was she? She loved him. But was she in love with him? Was she ready for something so consuming? "I'm telling you that I'm not going to turn to some other man when you're fifty-seven and I'm thirty-nine."

Still studying her, he nodded. "Okay."

Okay.

She'd parried. Offered a way out of a conversation that had gotten more personal than either one of them could handle.

And he'd accepted.

Then she remembered the bulimia. She couldn't keep doing this. Couldn't keep running. If she didn't face whatever was scaring her back into a physical disease she'd thought gone forever, she could end up dead.

But she wanted to lie back down. To pull Duane down with her. To cuddle up to his chest and know that she'd be safe there forever. Or at least until daylight took the sting of darkness away.

She sucked in as deep a breath as she could manage. "Now, let's hear worry number two."

CHAPTER SEVEN

WORRY NUMBER TWO. Duane didn't have them numbered. Or in any kind of order. They simply just popped up at will.

Like that damn brown bag still out on the porch. The one he hadn't touched. Or told her about.

"Kids is another one," he said, settling back against the bed, wishing he was dressed.

He'd be better at this with his pants on.

"Do you want to have kids?"

Feeling exposed wasn't something Duane did often. If at all.

"I'm assuming you want them, judging by how much time you spend with Phyllis's twins. How much you talk about them." Having kids was another subject they'd mostly avoided. It hadn't pertained to them in their safe little universe.

"I'm not ready to have children," she said slowly. "But you aren't, either. The next year's going to be crazy for you, with campaigning and your career. Then, assuming you win, which we both know you will, you'll have the added senate duties to consider. Certainly not a good time to think about doctor visits and building a nursery and birthing classes and midnight feedings."

He actually hadn't considered any of those things. Which probably proved her point.

"I'm not disagreeing with you," he said slowly. "But neither am I sure I'm going to want to become a father at fifty. Aside from all his friends thinking I'm his grand-father, I'm not sure it would be fair to the kid. I've already got bursitis in my elbow. Can you see me throwing a baseball ten years from now? Or running bases?"

"Who says he'll be a boy?"

"Softballs weigh more."

"So you're telling me you don't want kids?"

He wasn't telling her anything. She'd asked for worries. "I don't know," he finally said. "I've always wanted to be a dad, always thought I would be one. But the years have passed. I'm kind of like Becca. My goals are different. I don't want to be at risk for Alzheimer's when my child is a teenager and thinks he knows everything. Nor do I think it's fair to leave him hanging out there in his thirties when he needs business advice and I'm long gone."

Sophie didn't seem to have as easy an answer for this one. And they'd only just begun. Stumped at worry number two. That wasn't good.

He was going to lose her.

"Maybe we're going at this all wrong," Duane said, backpedaling as fast as he dared. "Analyzing too much. Trying to be too sure. How many marriages do you think would ever take place if the couples listed everything that could possibly go wrong before they got engaged?"

"Not as many, but I'd bet the percentage of successful unions would be up. Come on, Duane, you're in the business. You know as well as I do what the divorce rate in this country is."

Her words were offered matter-of-factly, but Duane wanted to kick himself for his stupidity. His insensitivity.

She was a product of divorce. Multiple divorces. Marriage, even one without potential issues, would be scary to her.

He'd missed this one. *And that, Counselor, is how you lose the most important case of your life.*

"I can promise you one thing, Sophie," he said seriously. "You aren't your mother, and neither am I. I don't take marriage lightly. Nor do I view it as expendable. If we do marry, it will be for keeps. I'm not going through another divorce. Living unhappily with the woman I love would be far better than that fight."

"All the more reason to make sure we aren't going to end up unhappy together, don't you think?"

"We're looking for guarantees that don't exist."

"No, we're looking at problems that do exist."

Her lack of emotion jarred him. And it dawned on him that she might be trying, Sophie-style, to break up with him.

"What's this really about?"

"I want to know what's different about you tonight."

Her gaze met his, steady and wide open. And he knew he had to give her the honesty she'd requested.

"A man was here."

"Where? In this bed? No way. Not unless you're talking about you."

"Not in this bed, Sophie, at this house."

Her frown seemed genuine. "Who? When?"

Just thinking about the casually dressed, gray-haired, athletic-looking guy caused Duane's blood pressure to rise. He should have kept this one to himself. All relationships had secrets.

Or so he'd heard from marriage counselors during client mediations.

Calm, buddy, he reminded himself. *You're overreacting.*

She's never given you any reason to think she'd be unfaithful to you.

On the contrary, Sophie went out of her way to pander to a jealousy he hadn't known he possessed before he met her.

A jealousy he wasn't proud of.

She was constantly reassuring him. Answering his questions even when he overstepped the bounds of their relationship.

"I don't know who," he said, trying to think about the case he'd won on Friday. The cocktail party he'd attended the night before. Racquetball. "He was here tonight. Before you got home." Even as he gave her the details, he suspected he was blowing this. There probably was a perfectly logical, sane explanation.

Still, why would a woman who lived alone allow an acquaintance to develop to the point of him knowing her schedule? Her address? And her favorite cookie?

And why hadn't she told Duane?

He stopped, not proud of what he was doing to himself. And to her.

Feeling stupid as hell, ashamed and immature, he shook his head. "I don't know who he was—he didn't give his name. Just said that he knew you were due back today and he wanted to leave a welcome-home gift."

She stared at him. "He left something? Where is it?"

"Where he left it. On the front porch."

With a frown, Sophie gave Duane one backward glance as she slid from the bed. She didn't look his way again as she pulled on the sweats and T-shirt hanging on the back of the bathroom door, and went to retrieve her gift.

Leaving him alone in her bedroom.

JAMES BENSON HAD LEFT HER a plate of chocolate-chip cookies with a simple note attached: "Welcome home." Followed by his signature.

It was very sweet of him.

And Sophie wished he hadn't done so.

"Who's James Benson?" Duane had followed her and now read over her shoulder. His tone was more congenial than accusatory.

And generic as hell.

"A neighbor."

"He drove here."

She stood, holding the brown bag at her side, and faced the man she'd been sleeping with for two years. She should have told Duane about James. She would have, if she hadn't been so worried that he'd think the wrong thing.

"He lives on Cactus Blossom." She pointed toward the street behind her, beyond the six-foot-high block-and-stucco fence that surrounded her backyard, feeling sick again. "That's his house on the opposite side of the wall."

"Why have I never seen him before, or even heard of him?"

A fair question from a man who had a key to her home. And a right to her bed.

"He's a winter renter. It's his first time in Shelter Valley."

"So you've only known him a few weeks."

"Yes."

"And you're already on friendly enough terms that he knows your schedule?" Duane's questions were numerous, but his tone didn't suggest anything other than casual interest.

Neither did his stance. Or the expression on his face.

There was nothing about him to instill the tension building in her stomach. He wasn't a violent man; she wasn't the least bit afraid of him. At least, not physically.

His ability to damage her heart was another matter.

"There was a leak in his irrigation system and it flooded my yard. He came over to let me know that it had been taken care of. To apologize. And to let me know that his insurance would cover any damage I incurred. We've talked over the fence a couple of times since, and I ran into him at the grocery store once."

"Has he ever been inside this house?"

"Or course not."

"Have you ever been to his place?"

Would Duane question any other woman this way? A woman who didn't have Sophie's past? "No."

"That still doesn't explain how he knew your schedule."

"He asked me what I do. I told him. He said it sounds like I travel a lot. I said yes and told him that I was leaving on a two-week trip. He offered to keep an eye on the place for me while I was gone."

"Does he have a key?"

"Absolutely not." The question bordered on inappropriate for what it implied about Sophie, except that in Shelter Valley, it wasn't uncommon for neighbors to have keys to each other's houses for emergency purposes.

"But he knows you live alone."

"Him and just about every one else in this town." One of the hazards of being single.

A light was shining from the house behind hers. James had said he had trouble sleeping. And now he'd know that Sophie was up, too. At three in the morning.

Did he also know that Duane was still there?

Not that it mattered. A select few of her friends knew that Duane stayed with her sometimes.

So why did she care what James Benson would think? Like her reputation suddenly mattered?

Like she was some innocent young thing needing protection?

Standing in front of her lover, Sophie realized that James made her feel like that young thing she'd never been.

And she didn't altogether hate the feeling. As if she could go back, relive her childhood, become the girl she wished she'd been.

Though it was far too late for her to have that kind of reputation, time didn't stop her from wanting it.

Duane caught her eye as she looked away from the backyard, then he glanced in that direction.

He probably noticed what she had—that James was either asleep with the lights on or he was up, too.

Duane turned back to her, standing tall, hands in his pants pockets. "I think you should end the friendship," he said quietly.

No.

The intensity of her first, thankfully silent reaction surprised her. She had no interest in James other than friendship. The man was close to sixty years old. But somehow, in the past weeks, his friendship had grown to matter to her. Had become a part of her home.

"Why?"

"You're my woman. My lover."

"We're lovers, yes."

"We're talking about getting married."

"What does that have to do with James?"

"The man brought you home-baked cookies. A man doesn't do that unless he's interested in a woman."

"Neighbors do."

"Female neighbors. With other females. And usually the one who's lived in the neighborhood a while brings them to the newcomer as a welcome gesture."

Sounded as though he'd given this a lot of thought. And since James had been by earlier, that would mean Duane had been having all of these thoughts while he'd been with her, proposing to her…

"Is that why you didn't accept my refusal of your proposal tonight like you usually do? Because you thought you had competition?"

Not a good reason to marry. At all.

"No!"

"Are you sure about that?"

"Absolutely. I told you, I've been thinking about this, about now being the right time, ever since you left."

"I wish I could believe you."

"Do I have competition?"

"How can you even ask that?"

Duane nodded toward the bag clutched at her side. "He's bringing you cookies."

Yeah, the cookies were a bit much. More than she'd have expected from the brief, friendly encounters.

"He's just a nice older guy, new to the area and alone. Shelter Valley's kind of intimidating at first. You know that. Everyone's friends with everyone, which makes an outsider feel…left out. And as for the cookies, maybe he's a chef or something."

"You don't know what he does for a living?"

"No. I'm assuming, since he's here for the winter, that he's retired. But I didn't ask."

She'd been friendly. Not encouraging.

"Where's he from?"

"Someplace back east. Maryland, I think." She didn't like how Duane was standing way over there, with his arms crossed over his still-bare chest.

Closed off.

As they'd been much of the time since he'd left her bed.

As he'd been?

But she didn't really want him over here right now, either.

"Does he have family? Kids?"

Sophie didn't want to answer. Duane seemed to be trying to trap her into admitting that she knew more about the man than she'd let on. That she knew him better than she'd said.

"I have no idea. He's never mentioned any kids."

"So he's not in a relationship?"

Confused, hating the interrogation even while, on some level, she understood it, even suspected she'd be asking the same sorts of things if the situation was reversed, Sophie replied, "He hasn't said and I haven't asked. But since he's here alone for the winter, I'm guessing not."

"Does he know about me?"

"He knows I'm seeing somebody." Which was more than Annie had known. Or anyone else outside of Shelter Valley.

Duane's gaze was piercing. "Seeing somebody. Is that all we're doing here? Seeing each other?"

He sounded hurt. And accusatory, in his quiet, unemotional way.

He was a master attorney, knew how to get the truth out of people on the stand.

But she wasn't a criminal.

"What did you want me to say, Duane?" Sophie cried out, when she wanted so badly to be as controlled as he was. Why did she have to care so much? "Did you want me to tell him that I've been seeing Duane Koch, the well-known attorney from Phoenix and possible senatorial candidate, exclusively for two years? Or maybe that I've been sleeping with a man who lives and works in Phoenix who largely keeps me a secret from his world? How about, I've dedicated my life to a man who comes to my small town to screw me, then goes merrily back to his own life without me? Or, wait, maybe I should say he's a man old enough to be my father who doesn't trust me and is ashamed of me. Would that do?"

His silence unnerved her more than anything. Her own words reverberated back at her, hurting her as much as he'd done with his interrogation and innuendos.

"This man, this James, does he make you feel better about yourself than I do?"

Was Duane finally beginning to understand? Could he get that she liked being liked for herself, not because she was an available body? Or was this going in another direction? Another way to trap her into admitting something that didn't exist?

"Yes," she told him honestly, because that was all she could be with Duane. No matter what happened, she couldn't cheapen with lies whatever it was they shared.

She would have expounded on that yes, explained how and why being around James was something she needed, except that she didn't understand the situation herself. She barely knew the man, and had no need to change that, but his seemingly no-strings-attached kindness, his acceptance of her occasional and completely generic conversation, his total disregard for her sexuality were good for her damaged soul.

"I want you to stop seeing him." Duane's quiet words were delivered in a tone that left no room for discussion.

It was the first time in their relationship that he'd ever talked down to her. Or that she'd felt any inkling of his doing so.

And her reaction was swift. Definite. "No."

He straightened, shoulders back, head a bit higher. "Really."

The effectiveness of that single word was amazing. She felt about two feet high.

But she withstood his stare anyway.

Loved him anyway. Even with ultimatums coming out of his mouth, he was Duane, the man she'd spent two years making love with. She might not be familiar with his home or his life outside of hers, but she knew him.

Duane didn't like being vulnerable. She understood that. And in a sense, he was facing his own mortality. Facing the fact that he was too old to have a relationship with a twenty-eight-year-old woman without explaining it. Facing the fact that he was getting too old to start a family.

"Let me get this straight," he said. "The man you say you love, who you want in your life, in your bed, asks you not to continue a friendship with a man you've just met, a man who's possibly already a little too fond of you, and you say no? Point-blank?"

"You have a huge piece of my heart, Duane, but you don't own my life. I don't even know most of the people you associate with every day. I've never met your partners, your neighbors. I've never even seen the inside of your condo—" though he'd driven her by it once when he'd picked her up from the airport "—yet you want me to let you choose my friends? To dictate to me? I can't let you do that."

"Or is it that you can't say no to any man who's kind to you?"

The words, cutting so completely into places already far too insecure, were Sophie's breaking point. She couldn't stand here. Couldn't take the pain he inflicted, knowingly or not. Couldn't fight with him.

She couldn't take on this man and win. Didn't even want to win.

She simply wanted to love and be loved.

With a bowed head, she returned to her room. Quietly and carefully she set the rest of Duane's clothes in the hall, then closed the door and locked it.

He had a key to the house. He could let himself out.

CHAPTER EIGHT

"Soph? Let me in." Duane rattled the door handle. He was due in court in just under two hours. She probably didn't know it, but the suit he'd brought with him was hanging in her closet.

A good excuse, but not the reason why he was still, an hour after she'd left the room, trying to get her to unlock the bedroom door.

He had time to drive home. Had a closetful of other suits. But he couldn't leave Sophie. Not like this.

Not with those horrendous words hanging between them.

He hadn't meant them.

At least not much.

He didn't want to mean them. Wasn't proud of the negative emotions that reared inside him where Sophie and other men were concerned.

"Sophie? I'm sorry, sweetie. I'm a fool who's feeling his age. Please, open the door."

Complete and utter silence met his plea. As it had met every other attempt he'd made to reach her.

He could pick the lock. They both knew that. All it took was a paper clip. He'd done it once, when Sophie had run from him in a burst of teasing foreplay, and told him he'd have to break in to catch her. It had taken him all of thirty seconds, and most of that had been eaten up with retrieving the paper clip.

He leaned his back against the door and crossed his arms.

He could call in to court, ask for a continuance on the case due to personal emergency. It would be the first time he'd done so in the twenty years he'd been practicing family law. Or he could call the office and have someone cover for him. A couple of the other attorneys knew the details of this morning's trial.

But he'd never done that before, either.

He could leave right now, arrive home in time to shower, dress, grab breakfast on his way to the office to pick up files, and still make it to court on time.

The latter seemed to be what she wanted. And definitely was the easiest choice—if he didn't consider the emotional ramifications inherent in leaving things this way.

He'd learned in the past two years that when things weren't right with Sophie, nothing else in his day unfolded smoothly. It was like coming upon a traffic light with purple, blue and black lights in a horizontal row rather than a vertical one. You knew you had to stop or slow down or continue through the intersection, but you had no way of deciphering which action you were to take when.

And that was how he felt. At an intersection in his life with circumstances that left him ignorant, yet requiring a decision.

And if he made the wrong choice, his life as he knew it could be over. Or he could kill someone—something—else.

If he hadn't already.

"Soph? Please."

Still no response. He should just go. This was her home. She'd made her wishes clear. He had to respect them.

Respect *her.*

"Soph? I'm going to come in to make certain you're all right, then I'll leave. You don't have to say anything, or even look at me, I just need to know you're okay."

Not a sound came in response.

With the paper clip he'd had in his hand for the past hour, Duane opened the door.

Sophie sat in the rocker in the corner of the room, holding a burnt-orange throw pillow against her stomach, staring out the window, where dawn was starting to light the sky.

She had to have heard him, but she didn't move, didn't acknowledge his presence.

It took everything he had not to go to her. To feel her skin, to connect with her warmth in whatever way he could.

He'd told her he'd go. So now he had to do so.

"I'll call you."

He wasn't even sure she heard the words. She didn't blink. Or react in any way.

And Duane wondered if maybe things were happening as they were meant to. Perhaps fate was intervening on her behalf. Because he wasn't sure, even as he hurt for her—and for himself—that if she threw herself into his arms, he'd have what it took to see them beyond all the strikes against them. He wasn't sure he'd ever believe in them enough to let her step away from him with the confidence that she'd always come back.

He wasn't sure that he wanted her in Phoenix, considering the price he could pay to have her there. An entire life's work lost.

Still, he couldn't end it with her.

By the time he arrived back in Phoenix, having spent the entire drive trying to make logical sense out of illogical emotions, Duane figured one thing. Being with a woman eighteen years younger than him was going to kill him.

IT WOULD HAVE BEEN BETTER if she didn't have the day off. She would have had to get out of the chair sooner—would have had to move sooner. As it was, Sophie sat until the sun was well and truly up. Sat long enough for Duane to have made it back to Phoenix.

Long enough for Phyllis to have gotten the twins to school and be in her office.

Then Sophie rose and found her phone.

"Hey, girl, I hope this means you're back in town safe and sound." Phyllis's voice greeted her after the first ring.

Sometimes caller ID was nice.

"Yeah, I'm back. And missing those babies." Calvin and Clarissa might be pushing seven, but Sophie suspected they'd still be her babies when they were twenty-seven. "Can I pick them up after school?" She could sure use a dose of their energetic chatter, innocent enthusiasm and honest views of the world.

"Of course. They'd love to see you. They're not out until four today. They're staying for arts and crafts— pottery is on the agenda."

"Can I keep them for dinner?"

"Better yet, why don't we all have dinner together? Matt put chili in the slow cooker before he left for work this morning."

Sophie loved chili. And she didn't dare be alone at mealtime. Not today.

"That'd be great, if you're sure I'm not imposing."

"Uh-oh. What's wrong?"

"What do you mean?"

"You've never been an imposition. How could you be? You're a part of our family, a part of Matt and me. But when you start thinking you are, that means you aren't feeling good about yourself."

Being friends with a psychologist, even a teaching one, was a blessing and a curse.

"I think we need to talk," Sophie said.

"I'm beginning to think so, too. I have classes and meetings all day, but I can cancel if it's an emergency."

"It's not."

"So tonight after dinner is soon enough?"

"That'd be great."

"You sure it'll wait?"

Sophie felt a little better already. "Yep."

"Okay, until then, take care of you, my friend."

"I will."

"You promise?"

"Yes, ma'am."

"Hey, Soph?"

"Yeah?"

"I'm glad you're home. We missed you."

"I missed you, too."

SOPHIE WAITED TO MAKE the second call until after she'd showered. She had about a ten-minute window to catch him in his car en route to court.

"Duane Koch." He sounded distracted. Either he hadn't looked at the caller ID on his cell or he was playing cold and distant with her.

"Hey."

"Soph? Where are you?"

"At home."

"Have you showered?"

"Yeah."

"You have plans this morning?"

"Just some calls to return. And a tape to watch for the Colorado show." Her upcoming March trip.

"Meet me for lunch?"

Had he read her mind? "Okay."

"At the southeast court complex in Mesa at eleven-thirty?" Not at the little diner halfway between Phoenix and Shelter Valley. Their usual spot.

Why?

She didn't have the emotional energy to ask. Wasn't sure she wanted to know. "Okay."

"You know how to get here?"

She'd been with him for two years and didn't have directions to the place where he spent a good number of his days. "I'll look it up on the Internet."

"Pull into the parking lot out front. I'll find you."

Don't come inside, where someone might see you with me, she translated.

"I'll be there."

For better or worse.

THE METAL IN HIS POCKET wasn't as precious as the ring he'd carried the day before. But Duane had an idea he was more on track with this one.

He'd rushed things.

Hard to believe, after two years of bedding the woman, that anything could be rushed, but he'd realized this morning that he'd lost Sophie's trust by acting so out of character the day before, pushing the marriage thing. She couldn't be expected to jump off the deep end when she hadn't yet learned to swim.

And he couldn't be expected to do so, either. He'd scared himself.

Stupid analogy, but after his sleepless night, and a challenging morning in court, it was the best he had.

He felt like a schoolkid as he rode the elevator down from the fourth-floor courtroom, impatient as it stopped at each floor, having to force the small talk with various legal persons of his acquaintance as they got on and off.

Would she really be there? Or would she have thought better of having accepted his invitation and left a message for him at the office instead?

Juggling his briefcase and keys, Duane grabbed his cell phone from the case on his belt. No messages. He dialed his office and tapped a foot while he waited for the phone to connect, all the while smiling and nodding at the people around him.

Finally, he landed on the ground floor, had to wait for the ten people in front of him to meander off. He punched in the code to his office message-retrieval system.

There were five calls. One of his partners. *Skip.* A political acquaintance. *Skip. Skip. Skip.* Nothing from Sophie.

Because…

There she was. With the beautiful Arizona sun shining down on that gorgeous blond head, waiting outside her Explorer. She was wearing black jeans, with the high-heeled leather boots she'd had on the night they'd met. And the black sweater he'd bought for her for her birthday.

Seeing him, she climbed inside her truck, started it up. A quick getaway? Did she intend to follow him? Or think he wanted her to?

Was she telling him she was going to drive?

Duane ignored his Mercedes. He walked to the passenger side of her truck and knocked on the window. She rolled it down.

"Hey, babe. You look gorgeous."

Her smile was passive. "Thank you."

"Unlock this thing, will you?"

She glanced around, then back at him. With a shrug, she did as he asked.

Because he always drove when they were together, Duane had only been in her truck a handful of times—and always in the driver's seat. But he managed to climb in and buckle his belt without mishap.

"I thought you'd want me to follow you."

"You mind driving?" he asked, as if they did this sort of thing every day. Perhaps he was being unfair. He simply couldn't afford to make it easy for her to reject him.

"You want me to drive?" Her words were as much statement as question.

"If you don't mind."

With one more perplexed look in his direction, Sophie put the truck in Reverse and backed out of her parking spot. "Where are we going?"

He named the intimate lunch pub he'd chosen.

"I thought we'd do a drive-through and go to a park or something."

"You don't like the restaurant?"

"No, it's fine."

For the remainder of the trip she silently followed his directions.

Duane didn't think, even for a second, that the rest of the time they had together would go so easily.

Or that she'd capitulate so readily.

The back of his neck started to ache. When Sophie clammed up like this it meant she had something to say. He only hoped he got the chance to speak first.

CHAPTER NINE

HER STOMACH SETTLED for the first time that morning, merely having him close. Didn't matter that they weren't speaking. That they had problems that might be bigger than they were. Not as she followed Duane into one of her favorite restaurants.

Nothing seemed to matter but that she was close to him. With him.

Probably because she needed sleep. And was scared about the bulimia.

She didn't have the flu. No fever. No lack of appetite. And she couldn't possibly be pregnant. She and Duane used a condom every single time. No mistakes. No close calls.

She'd wondered if she had an ulcer, but there was no burning, or pain in her stomach.

As if by some unspoken agreement, their silence continued until they'd ordered. Duane tried to talk her into a barbecue ranch chicken sandwich. She chose the salad version instead. And a diet soda.

But promised herself she'd eat every bite. And she'd eat the bread that came with the salad, too. With butter.

And at some point she was going to tell her lover that she had to quit seeing him for a while. At least until she got herself under control. Until she could trust herself to deal with the challenges he posed in her life, and stay healthy at the same time.

"Thank you for agreeing to lunch." Duane's words were soft, his gaze open and sincere.

"I was planning to ask you to lunch anyway," she said. She'd hoped to eat before they had this discussion. Worst case, if their talk disrupted her meal, she could always get something on the way home. And if that failed, she'd be having dinner with the Sheffields that night.

Which meant she'd be eating well no matter what.

Sophie's breath caught when Duane took her hand. She braced herself. If he put a ring on her finger, she'd give it back. She had to break up with him. Couldn't let him get to her, couldn't let herself be weak or back down.

The past had taught her well.

Taking care of her health came first. Without that, there would be no life ahead. As things currently stood, Duane was detrimental to her health.

"Soph…this morning… I'm so sorry."

"It's okay." And it was, as far as his culpability was concerned. He'd only been speaking the truth, which she'd asked him to do.

"No, it's not okay." His tone changed. "I was a guy being a guy in every bad sense of the word."

Sophie had her plan. She knew what she was in Phoenix to do. But that didn't stop her from needing to listen to what Duane had to say.

"I'm a man of words," he continued, still holding her hand as they sat across from each other in the booth.

She'd have to pull that hand away. Soon.

"I know the power of words," he said. "Words can send a man, or woman, to prison for life."

"Their actions do that," she said, before he could lock himself up and throw away the key due to a statement she'd practically asked him to make.

He thought she was one of those women. The kind who gave their bodies like most people gave smiles. He thought she'd trade her body for kind words. That she couldn't help but do so. He thought what he thought because she'd once *been* that kind of woman.

"Yes, but beyond their actions, or even their guilt, so many times, it's the words an attorney chooses that sway a jury. Words convince jurors of the guilt or innocence of a defendant," he said. "And sometimes, in everyday life, words have long-reaching consequences, too. Sometimes something that's said out of emotional reaction does permanent damage."

She wanted to argue. To assure him no harm had been done. *Or is it that you can't say no to any man who is kind to you?*

But harm had been done.

Their salads arrived and Sophie pulled her hand free to spread her napkin on her lap. Then kept her free hand in her lap as she picked up her fork.

"I'm sorry, Sophie. I would give anything to be able to take the words back. I didn't mean to hurt you."

But did you mean what you said?

They had a problem that wasn't going to go away.

This had nothing to do with love. It had to do with being human—with two people who had human weaknesses that didn't coexist well.

"You spoke the truth," she said. The lettuce on her fork was not finding its way to her mouth. "You can't be blamed for that."

"I spoke the jealous words of an insecure older man," he said. "Not the truth. There was no thought, no truth anywhere in that moment."

Accepting the explanation he was offering was so tempting. She needed to believe that his last statement in their predawn confrontation had been no more than an insecure outburst.

So why had it reflected exactly what she'd told Annie two nights ago?

Annie. A different life. Separate from Duane and all the pain. The fear.

"You don't trust me, or trust my moral makeup." She still held the forkful of salad. It seemed necessary somehow.

Duane wasn't eating, either. He wasn't even pretending to eat. "That's not true," he said softly, yet somehow managed to sound so firm, so sure. "You aren't the problem. I am."

"Why? Because you aren't willing to calmly accept that your girlfriend had a tendency to go to bed with various men in a quest for acceptance?"

Sophie had been looking for love her whole life. And eight years ago, she'd thought she'd found it inside herself. But present circumstances were jeopardizing that belief.

She had to find that love inside herself again. That was the only way to stay healthy. According to Phyllis and to every self-help book, pamphlet and article Sophie had read.

She could think through every aspect of her life now, every role she played, and know that she wasn't wholly dependent on any one of them. Each person, each relationship played a part. And only a part.

She was the only constant.

"I don't have a girlfriend who had the tendency to be

with various men," Duane said quietly. "I have a lover who was once a lost child seeking comfort the only way she knew how."

Sophie tried not to be touched by his words. Maybe she'd been baiting him with that last statement.

Maybe she'd been baiting him for a while.

Maybe she was pushing him away because their relationship wasn't working for her anymore. The world had entered their private chamber and what once was perfect and clear had become too messy for her.

He was starting to spill over into other aspects of her life. More, she was starting to spill over into his.

"What I have is a jealous streak that I didn't know existed, and that I'm not proud of," Duane said. "I've never found myself in a position where I lack confidence. With you, I do."

Don't do this, Sophie begged silently, setting down her fork and clasping her hands in her lap. *Don't pull me back in. Don't make it impossible for me to walk away.*

Don't make me fall completely in love with you.

"You're eighteen years younger than I am, Soph. And absolutely gorgeous. Men stare at you everywhere we go. Stare at you as though they'd like to know you better. Men with much more to offer you than I have. Men with youth and looks and a body that isn't yet showing the signs of aging, sprouting wrinkles or producing random aches and pains. Men who aren't yet turning gray. Men who don't have to have their blood pressure checked regularly, or care so much about yearly screenings and cholesterol. At some point, one of those men is going to be bold enough to issue an invitation that you might not want to pass up."

"Because I'm loose and open to that, you mean?"

"No. Because you're human and we're naturally attracted to beauty. It's a given that if you put two centerfolds in a roomful of women, one who is virile and young and cover-model material, and one who is older and not as firm, and wrinkled and gray, they would find the first one more attractive."

"So you think physical attraction is everything," Sophie said, turning the table on him from last night's conversation. "That's why you're with me, a woman eighteen years younger than you are. Because of my physical attributes. Because a woman your age would be not as firm, and starting to wrinkle, with hair that's turning gray."

"No. I'm with you because your eyes draw me in every single time I look at you. Because when you speak, I can't help but listen, because I'm enthralled by whatever it is you have to say. Because where most people bore me eventually, you keep me mentally stimulated. I like how you think. I like that random things amuse you. I'm addicted to your compassion, your acceptance of other people in spite of their shortcomings. I like how you always take the side of the underdog. At least at first."

He was giving her what she'd given him the night before. As sincerely? He was sucking her back in.

"I've been with men before," she said. "Great-looking men. And I know for absolute certain that it's not just a body that turns me on. I'd be perfectly fine never having another man in my life, if he's there just for sex. I've got news for you, Duane. I don't live for sex. Other than with you, I've never found that making love was anything like it's built up to be. In fact, it was far, far less. So take that to your old and wrinkled chamber and sit with it for a while."

"I just stepped into crap again, didn't I?"

Their waitress stopped by, eyed the untouched plates. "Is everything all right?"

"Fine," Duane said in a polite tone that was dismissive enough to regain their privacy. Then he looked Sophie straight in the eye.

"I'm the older one here," he said. "At my age I'm supposed to know better than to jump to conclusions, or react emotionally before thinking. I should have all the answers. Or at least more of them. So why do I feel as though I'm twenty again, experiencing love for the first time?"

His words made her smile—inside and out. In spite of all that she knew, all she had to protect, to be aware of, to tend to. "I don't know. Why do you?" she asked, when she wasn't supposed to engage.

"Because I *am* up against love for the first time." Duane looked rather uncomfortable with the admission.

She wanted to reach for his hand. "Funny how years only make you wise when you live them fully and have different types of experiences," she said. "You want to be mature and savvy when it comes to having a long-term relationship with a woman, yet it's not anything you've got much experience with."

"And what makes you so wise?"

"I'm not. I'm simply on the outside looking in on this one." Her smile faded. "But I'm no better off. I don't know what to do with us, either. I just know I can't lose myself in you," Sophie continued. She was here to end things, at least for a time. She couldn't let herself down. "I can't give up me, or become someone I'm not." She said aloud a truth she'd paid dearly to learn. "I can't suddenly keep to myself and quit being friendly with people, quit knowing people, because it might make you jealous."

"I'm not asking you to."

"You did last night." And he would again. And she would overcompensate by keeping herself slim and beautiful, by seeing her worth in her body, her looks, so that, if she was left alone again, she could find someone to share her life with. So that people would notice her. Like her. And she wouldn't be all alone.

She couldn't go down that road again.

The time had come. She had to end this.

Taking a deep breath, she tried to choose her words carefully, kindly.

"I have a proposal," Duane said.

"I know. You made that clear last night, but—"

His shaking head stopped her. Confused her in the midst of finding the inner strength to walk away from a man who'd come to mean more to her than was healthy.

She couldn't depend on a man—any man—for her emotional well-being.

"Hear me out, okay? Then see what you think."

Because a part of her welcomed the interruption, welcomed delaying that last moment she'd see his face, welcomed not having to choose between him and fighting the recurrence of her near-fatal disease, Sophie nodded.

HE WAS LOSING HER. Duane was not a stupid man. He could read the signs. The distant look in her eyes. The hands kept safely out of reach. The food that hadn't been touched.

But, believing in his case, he pushed forward anyway.

Or perhaps desperation drove him. He couldn't live without her. In spite of the fact that he wasn't sure he could live with her.

He was being unfair.

And knowing that didn't stop him.

"I'm not a perfect man, or even an easy one, Sophie, but I want you in my life. I need for you to be happy, I need to be able to make you happy, in order for me to be happy."

"I—"

He held up a hand. "Let me finish, and then I'll listen to, and abide by, whatever you have to say. Okay?"

She nodded.

"I'm not going to sit here and promise you that I'll never get jealous again. While I am beginning to accept that this green-eyed monster has appeared as part of the package of being with you, I recognize that I'm far too inexperienced to know how to beat him. I am not confident yet that I've won that particular fight.

"I'm also not going to tell you that I think it can be smooth sailing ahead for us. I can't. I simply don't know. I'm beginning to suspect I have very few answers for us. But this I do know. I can't give up on us."

Tempted to leave it there, to pretend that he'd said all he'd originally intended to say, Duane paused. Yet in spite of himself, in spite of his fears, he had to go on.

"I've made some major mistakes here, Soph. And one of them I can, with your willingness and cooperation, correct. I'd like for us to try." He was running around the block, conversationally speaking, to avoid arriving at his destination.

What if she didn't agree? He didn't have another plan waiting. Another defense.

What if she did agree? He'd have to follow through.

Or lose her.

"We jumped straight from acquaintances to lovers to needing to be together without actually sharing our lives," he said. "We share moments in each other's lives. Period."

"Exactly." She sat back, arms crossed at her chest again. Closing him off?

"By keeping our relationship mostly a secret, I thought I was protecting us. Giving us a chance to find out who and what we were together before we had to fight the low opinions of others. I was protecting your reputation. And—" he took another deep breath "—protecting my own, as well."

"And it worked," Sophie said. "For a while. But what we have isn't real, Duane. At least not in a daily life sense. What we have can't stand the test of a career move, let alone anything really going wrong. What if one of us got sick? What if you were in an accident? Who would know to contact me? And even if someone did, unless you were conscious, I wouldn't be able to sit by your side, to ask doctors about your condition. As far as almost anyone in your life knows, I don't exist."

"I'm getting to that." Leaning back, he reached into his pocket. Pulled out the small piece of metal and set it on the table. "When I proposed to you last night, I meant every word. I want us to be together. But the proposal was ill-timed. Unfair. Mostly to you. We've skipped necessary steps. The getting-to-know-all-aspects-of-each-other steps. The entering-each-other's-lives steps. What I'm proposing today is that we take those steps."

She was staring at the table. "I don't understand. What does that mean?" Her voice shook, and he couldn't tell whether it was from excitement, nervousness or fear.

Maybe all three.

Lord knew, he'd run the gamut. Several times. In the past five minutes alone.

"I want for us to start sharing our lives. That's a key to

my condo. I should have given it to you the day I accepted the key to your home. I want you to take it."

She left it lying on the table.

"I don't want you to just carry the key on your ring in case of an emergency or something, Sophie. I want you to use it. I want my home to become your home, like yours has become mine."

"You think sleeping at your place sometimes is going to solve all this?"

"No. I'm not talking about hiding out here as well as in Shelter Valley," he said. But he couldn't blame her for thinking so. "I'm not talking about hiding out at all."

He'd been a selfish, pompous, all-knowing ass. Hope to God it didn't cost him his ass.

"I'm proposing that we live together." Out loud, the words sounded so much worse, so much more risky. "As you said last night, we have a lot of challenges ahead. And neither one of us is willing to consider divorce. But it would be equally criminal for us to lose this chance because of things we can't predict. Who knows how people will react to us until we give them a chance? Who knows how we'll feel when they do react? Who knows any of the answers to the very hard and real challenges facing us unless we at least try to face them?"

"You want us to live together."

"Yes. However that works for us. A few nights a week here, or maybe when I have to be in court early in the mornings. Weekends and other nights in Shelter Valley. And when you're on the road, I'll take care of both places."

There's no way another bastard is going to be looking out for my woman.

Shut up, man.

Even now, the fight raged within Duane. At least this time he had the discipline to keep the thought to himself.

And yet it wasn't completely wrong. He and Sophie were lovers. He had the right to care for her. And needed to be the one she relied upon.

That was normal. Natural. Healthy…

"Say something." He finally broke the silence that was giving far too much free rein to his mind at a time when his heart was so vulnerable.

"I—"

"If it doesn't work, I won't push things."

"I…"

She what? Didn't love him? Or not enough?

"I…"

She couldn't seem to find any words. But she reached over, picked up the key and slid it into a side pocket of her purse.

CHAPTER TEN

"So you think I'm being an idiot?" Sophie glanced sideways as she walked beside Phyllis. The eye contact was important. Sophie's days of being an ashamed and embarrassed college girl were over.

"Of course I don't," Phyllis said, her smile as warm and genuine as always. The two women were halfway around the mile block they'd chosen for this evening's exercise, while Matt stayed behind to bathe the twins and read bedtime stories.

"Do you think I made the right choice not to break up with him?" Sophie had confessed everything, from the first bout of nausea two nights before, to her silent acceptance of Duane's key that afternoon.

"I think only you can determine that," Phyllis said, her confident voice ringing clearly. "Relationships don't come with an owner's manual, Soph. What's right for some isn't right for others. It's all a matter of personal choice based on what works for you."

"But if being with him is making me sick, if it's bringing back the eating disorder—"

"Then you need to tend to the eating disorder."

Phyllis's hand brushed Sophie's as they turned a corner, and the contact calmed a bit of the panic that had been dogging her since her trip to the Sheffields' bathroom after dinner.

"You know full well that you don't get healthy by running away. You sure couldn't change your mother's lifestyle, your upbringing or your teenage years the last time you struggled with this. You had to take charge of *you*." Phyllis's no-nonsense personality was impossible to ignore. Or doubt. "The disorder is a sign that there's something wrong within your psyche, Soph. It can be, and almost always is, stimulated by outward occurrences and situations, but the basic problem still remains within you.

"Breaking up with Duane might take care of the immediate symptoms, but it's not going to do a thing to cure the cause. To the contrary, it will probably enhance the problem, as that action is only going to make you feel worse than you do already. On some level, you would know that this relapse would have inadvertently caused you to be alone and to feel unloved again, which would only trigger more of that internal drive to take control of your life by controlling your appetite and your body's natural need for sustenance.

"Of course, that's assuming you truly want a relationship with him."

"I do." Sophie's response wasn't all that enthusiastic. And in the silence Phyllis always seemed to allow at the most painful times of self-discovery, Sophie thought of something else.

"But just because I want to be with Duane doesn't mean he's as certain he wants to be with me. Or that he wants the same things I do. What if I'm feeling bad because some part of me senses that he's using me? Or lying to me? What if I am only a fling to alleviate his midlife crisis? The young thing who reassures him he's still got it? As long as

I'm making him feel good about himself, he'd have a hard time getting rid of me, right? He'd still want me around."

Their steps had slowed, the rubber soles of their tennis shoes beating a sleepy rhythm against the cement.

"Is that what you are, Sophie? A pander to his ego? Is that what you allow yourself to be?"

"Of course I don't allow it. But I can't control him. I can't jump inside Duane's heart and make him feel differently."

"And he can't make you into something you are not. He can't make you into a bimbo who willingly serves his needs without holding him accountable to your needs, as well. Only you can allow that to happen."

There was something important here, if only Sophie could quit cycling through her panic and get it.

"If he's meeting my needs, it doesn't matter what others think."

"How you let others' opinions affect you is an entirely different matter," Phyllis replied as they turned another corner. "One we might need to pursue, mind you, but not what I'm talking about here. We know that the basis of your eating troubles stems from the way you view yourself."

"So if I'm feeling like a bimbo who allows Duane to use her without love, it's because I'm allowing him to do so."

"Or because you feel like you are a bimbo that a man would only use, not love."

"And if I knew I wasn't, then I wouldn't allow him anywhere near me if I wasn't sure that he loved me."

"Now you're getting it."

"This isn't about Duane at all."

"Nope."

Sophie had known that.

While Phyllis waved at Randi and Zack Foster, who

were driving by, Sophie's mind raced. "It's possible that he really does care."

"Yep."

"I'm not letting him in far enough to find out."

"That's my guess."

"It's me who still doesn't trust myself."

SOPHIE DIDN'T USE HER KEY Monday night. When Duane had climbed out of her truck at the courthouse that afternoon, he'd told her he had early court Tuesday morning. It had been understood between them for more than a year that early court meant he had to stay in Phoenix.

She'd nodded. Nothing more. And with his key in her pocket, she'd driven away.

She'd had a date with the twins. And dinner with their parents. He'd known that. And hadn't started hoping to hear her key in the lock until eight o'clock that night. And not seriously until nine.

At ten his cell phone rang. Her name flashed on the view screen.

"Where are you?" he asked, staring out the window, his heart pounding as he tried not to consider all the things that could happen to a young woman traveling across the dark desert at night.

"In my room, why?"

At home. In Shelter Valley. Not driving toward him. Not even attempting to get there. "You aren't coming."

"Not tonight."

Did that mean she was coming another night? Soon? Suddenly, in the face of the possibility that she actually might not use the key he'd so painstakingly given her, he wanted her to use it. Another vagary of life.

One hand jammed in his pants pocket, Duane paused. He didn't know what to say. How to make things right between them.

"I was going to break up with you today."

"You said *was*." Always the attorney, looking for angles. For the less obvious truth.

A less obvious truth like he was really falling in love with a twenty-eight-year-old woman.

"Phyllis and I talked tonight."

The psychologist had helped Sophie professionally in the past. And they'd been friends for years. Phyllis liked Duane. Didn't she? She'd sure seemed to. She was in pretty tight with Will's wife, Becca.

After a full minute passed, Duane realized Sophie hadn't said anything more. Dropping onto the home-theater-style sofa precisely positioned between the large screen and the speakers in his living room, he stared out at the darkness.

In another second or two he'd turn on a light.

Read some files.

"What did Phyllis have to say?" he finally asked.

"That I'm blaming you for things that I'm doing."

"She said that?"

"Not exactly. But it's what she wanted me to figure out for myself."

Afraid to know, Duane still had to ask. "What *are* you doing?" Being unfaithful when they weren't together? Getting bored with him?

"Assuming the worst and not asking for what I want."

Duane sat up straight. "What do you want?"

"I'm not sure. I just know I'm not ready to have you all over my life. To be all over yours."

"You don't love me."

"I'm not saying that."

"What are you saying?"

"I-I'm scared, Duane."

Okay. That he could understand. Sympathize with. But… "Do you want to break up with me?"

"No."

Duane thought about the women he'd known. He'd been circumspect, smart, but he was forty-six years old. He'd had lovers. With kindness. Respect. Precautions to health and the prevention of children. But with no thought of relationship beyond the moment.

Sophie was different.

"So what do you want?" he asked again, acknowledging that it mattered. A lot.

"Peace," she said. "And health."

She was losing him. "What does that mean in the context of us?"

"I'm not sure. Because of my own issues I'm struggling to keep up with us."

"How so?"

"The bulimia is back."

And that, Duane knew, was why she'd talked to Phyllis. Why Sophie was in Shelter Valley and not Phoenix.

A new dimension had been added to their problems. At a time when the challenges facing them were already too heavily weighted against them.

His heart ached for her. She was so beautiful. So kind and giving. Funny and smart. He didn't know many details of her history before arriving at Montford, but he knew that because a few people in her life had been too selfish to care for the child within her, to meet her basic needs, she now struggled to nurture herself.

Suddenly it didn't matter that she wanted to try to make things work with him—or he with her. It was a question of whether or not she was capable of doing so.

The stakes had changed. In an instant.

"Are you sure you aren't just stressed out and suffering from good old-fashioned nerves?"

She told him about the vomiting.

"Maybe you have the flu."

Then she told him about the fasting.

And the gorging she did at dinner that night.

She told him how much better she felt, emotionally, after she purged. Until the guilt set in, at which time she'd start to panic.

She seemed to give him every little ounce of ugliness she could find within her. And all he could see was her beauty—and the crime inherent in such an incredible human being having been so neglected that she couldn't see her own value.

Sophie Curtis's parents had much to answer for.

In the meantime, loving her meant giving her his strength when she'd hit her own personal wall. Letting her lean on him until she found her own strength. Just as she did for him every single time he doubted himself.

"We'll fight it together, Soph." The promise wasn't idle at all. "You're in control here. You know that. You've met this challenge head-on before and won. We'll do whatever you need. Take a break. Or not. Hide. Or not." He considered his career and started to sweat. He had to deal with his needs, too.

He'd find a way. Somehow. "Just don't shut me out." He was rambling now, even if it was the truth. She'd scared him, plain and simple. "Let me show you the Sophie I see.

The Sophie who has grown to mean so much to me. I promise you, once you meet her, you're going to see how great she is."

When Sophie chuckled, Duane started to breathe again. He'd overreacted. Because he cared. Really cared.

"I think it's pretty obvious I'm not going anywhere, Duane," she said, her voice husky and still a bit self-deprecating. "At least not right now. Apparently the onset isn't about you."

For which Duane was deeply thankful.

Their conversation eased into chatting about news headlines and the economy and things that touched them equally. Until both of them were falling asleep. And as he climbed into his king-size bed alone that night, Duane was content.

He might be in midlife and in a crisis, but it wasn't a midlife crisis. He wasn't fantasizing or lusting after youth. He had a lover whom he cared about a great deal.

He was glad to have that straight once and for all.

CHAPTER ELEVEN

"So what do you think? Can you make it rain on the stage for the entire number without ruining anything, and have the place ready for a ballet piece two minutes later?"

"Probably." Sophie frowned, studying the videotape of the act that would take place during the storm, as well as a site plan of the stage area itself. With the help of digital lighting and carefully orchestrated darkness and shadows she should create the appropriate atmosphere. Using clear tubing to contain the water, she could tap into the plumbing that ran from the dressing room stage left, under the stage, to dressing room stage right. Afterward the tubes could be pulled up to the ceiling, out of the way....

After relating the specifics to Matt Sheffield, the fine arts technical coordinator at Montford, Sophie concluded, "I saw something similar done in Utah several years ago. Of course, with our digital technology, we'll be able to create an effect that will convince even the Grinch that the heavens have opened at our command."

"And you have the time?"

She had another week before she had to leave for Colorado. After that... "The show's in March?"

"The second weekend, yes."

"Then I have the time." She could do fire, too. And make people fly, if he needed her to.

She just couldn't seem to trust herself to open up her life to someone, and not fall apart if a relationship failed.

To let her relationship with Duane progress beyond her comfort zone.

"Now for the really bad news." Wearing jeans that molded his long legs, a short-sleeved black shirt showing pecs that no man could be ashamed of and the rough-rider shoes that had become his signature, Matt told her what his budget would allow him to pay her.

She'd be working with his most promising students. Teaching. And spring was one of her busiest times, next to summer. And the holiday season.

"How about I do it for that and a favor?" she said.

"Of course. What do you need?"

"Some painful conversation."

When Matt leaned back slightly, his eyes narrowing, Sophie knew that some lessons were never forgotten. Some hurts remained for life.

"Painful how?"

"Painful to you in content, not in deed," she said. "Phyllis is the one who suggested I speak with you."

The wife he adored. The only woman Matt had ever really trusted. Or ever would trust, if Sophie had her guess.

He appeared to weigh his options, looking over the distant, empty stage from the sound booth where they stood. But Matt wasn't slow to make up his mind. He was probably trying to find the wherewithal to live up to another one of the challenges Phyllis continued to throw at him to help him stay fully, emotionally alive, engaged. Forcing him to face feelings that he'd spent a lifetime avoiding.

"Okay." He finally relented, still not looking at Sophie. "When?"

"Now."

That got his attention. His head swung toward her. "Why now?"

"Because I needed the answers last night."

"Can I get a cup of coffee first?"

"You got any juice in that vending machine of yours?"

"Unless the kids cleared it out. We rented this theater to one of those L.A. talent competitions last weekend. It's how I'm coming up with the funding for *Stormy Weather.*"

"You bring me juice, I'll wait for you to get your coffee," Sophie said.

"Two beverages coming right up." Matt turned back at the door. "By the way, what do you know about the guy who's renting behind you? I meant to ask Phyllis if she'd asked you, but forgot. Greg Richards said he saw you talking with him at the grocery store."

Greg Richards, Shelter Valley's sheriff.

After relating the little she knew about her temporary neighbor, she sat back to await Matt's return. She couldn't remember the times she'd waited in this exact sound booth, on this very same couch, for Matt to appear. Funny how she didn't feel any more confident now than she had then.

"So what's up?"

He handed her a plastic bottle of juice—lid already removed—then sipped from a steaming cup as he sat on the rolling chair in front of the control panel, facing her.

Looking at the man who'd once been all she could think about, all she'd fantasized about, Sophie opened her mouth to speak.

And half laughed instead. "Did I mention that this is going to be far more painful for me than for you?"

"I kind of figured so." The words didn't win her one of Matt's rare smiles. But then, with the years he'd spent in prison wrongly convicted of the rape of an underage girl, one of his students, he'd seen a lot more of the harsher side of life than she had. His walls were higher. More firmly in place.

And Sophie, a former student who'd once told others he was in love with her, would always pose a bit of a threat.

"Easiest way is to just get on with it," he said after a few more sips of coffee.

Right. She was twenty-eight, not twenty. And was lover to a man eight years older than Matt.

If that wasn't a bit weird.

Hands clasped around the bottle, Sophie stared at the tiled floor of the booth. "I need you to tell me, honestly, if you were ever the least bit attracted to me."

Matt's sigh was more telling than any words that might follow. She was, and always had been, a pain in his ass.

"Sophie, we've been through all of this before. You know that I never once gave you any reason to think that I wanted—"

"That's not what I asked," she said, meeting his gaze head-on. "I asked if you ever found me attractive. You know, looked at me and noticed that I had something to offer in the guy-girl department."

"What man alive with healthy testosterone wouldn't?" His tone was dry. "Except maybe one who's into obesity. And even then, if your body was plastered on a wall someplace, he might be tempted."

Just as she'd thought—as she'd tried to tell Phyllis the

night before: men looked at her and saw a slut. It had been that way since she was thirteen years old.

"But we're only talking about a body, Soph. Not a flesh-and-blood person. Not the woman who is sitting before me. And not the promising student you were before."

She listened because Phyllis had said it would do her some good. And because Sophie trusted her friend and wanted to do everything in her power to beat the menace inside her as quickly as possible.

"You've got a skewed perception of men," he continued, in the tone she'd once heard every day in the classroom. "Most men, decent men, don't only see a body when a woman walks into the room. And they don't mentally strip her, either. I'm not going to tell you it doesn't happen, because it does. But when it does, most men immediately shut down the image and move away. Unless there's more involved. Unless his attraction is appropriate and welcomed."

"Yours was welcomed."

"But not appropriate."

"So you weren't even the least bit tempted." Phyllis had told her to ask. As though Sophie needed this humiliating experience to somehow start liking herself. Or see herself differently.

"My wife knows we're having this conversation," he said, his gaze narrowed again.

"Yes."

"Do you mind if I call her to make certain?"

Sophie knew he didn't trust her. And didn't blame him. "No. I don't mind."

The first time she had met Phyllis, and several times after that, she'd talked to her about her supposed love affair with Matt.

He was off the phone in about ten seconds.

"You going to answer my question now?" Sophie asked, feeling sick to her stomach again. She was ready to get this over with and move on. Move out. Maybe even out of Shelter Valley. Arizona. Move to a place where no one knew her, or about her past. A place where she could be whoever she wanted to be without having to answer for things she couldn't change.

Or to keep paying for them.

Except that she couldn't move away from her own psyche. Her own fears. She couldn't move away from herself.

"The answer is yes."

She hadn't heard him right. Staring at Matt, Sophie waited for him to correct himself. To elaborate. To confirm that she'd misunderstood.

"You were," she said instead, her mouth dry. "Tempted, that is."

"Yes, I was tempted."

"To have sex with me."

"To get to know you better."

"In a sexual sense."

"In a man-woman sense."

She carefully set the bottle of juice on the floor, then propped herself up by planting a hand on either side of her, fighting dizziness.

Phyllis couldn't possibly know this. Otherwise she would never, ever, have had Sophie ask Matt.

"It's because I exude something you couldn't avoid," she elaborated for him. "Something naughty, a guy fantasy. Something that says I'm easy." She forced herself to hear the truth, as though the knowledge would somehow allow her to find a way to live with it and still live the kind of life she wanted. Or was she destined for a life where she had lots of different kinds of relationships, but where, ultimately, she was alone? Because she was afraid to depend too much on others for fear they'd leave, and she'd end up like her mother?

Out on the most precarious limb of her life, Sophie fought with everything she had to get through this moment to hang on to the deep level of trust she felt for Phyllis Sheffield. To hang to the hope that she could someday end up on the other side of this battle, married to a man she loved, with children to raise.

"Why were you tempted?" she asked again, when Matt continued to silently contemplate her.

"I was tempted because you were so sweet, so smart and so damned alone." He leaned forward, elbows on his knees. "I knew what alone was. I knew how it felt to be in Shelter Valley, surrounded by all of the love and family that flows so freely here, and not be a part of that."

Surely Phyllis had told him to say that. That was the only explanation for why he was saying what Sophie needed to hear.

Except Phyllis and Matt had been on the phone for a matter of seconds.

She must have told him the night before. Even though she'd said she wouldn't. Her first loyalty was to Matt, not Sophie....

"And...I was tempted by your adoration of me," he added.

Sophie stared at him, every muscle in her body frozen.

"Your affection wasn't contrived," he said, in a tone so simple, so natural, she accepted the truth in his words. It helped that she knew he was right. Her adoration for this man hadn't been anything like what she'd felt for those other men. Nor had it really been all that sexual.

Or maybe it had been. Sex was the only way she'd known to give affection.

"You weren't after a good grade, or anything I could do for you. You seemed to just care about me, the person. You cared whether I had enough to eat, whether another student had let me down. You cared that I was alone all the time."

She had cared. Too much. Far, far too much.

"You were the only person who saw how lonely I was. It was through your eyes that I saw myself."

"And Phyllis knows this."

"Phyllis has always said a prayer of thanks that you came into our lives. You, who thought you had so little worth that you were slowly killing yourself, taught us both how to trust, how to love. Without you in our lives, we might never have found each other, beyond that one moment of lust that gave us Calvin and Clarissa."

"But you didn't trust me enough, just now, to have this conversation without Phyllis knowing that we were talking."

"I didn't want to betray a confidence between my wife and me," Matt clarified. "I'd assured her that no one but her would ever know about that temptation in my life. The temptation of you. With my history, if this were to get out, there could be all kinds of misconceptions flying around."

As hard as she tried, Sophie couldn't stop the tears that slowly filled her eyes. "I can't believe you guys trust me that much."

"We made you guardian of Calvin and Clarissa in our wills."

"Yeah, but nothing's ever going to happen to the two of you, at least not until those babies are old and gray themselves and wheeling us all around, so that was kind of a moot point."

She took a sip of juice. A long sip. Finished off the bottle. Suddenly ravenous, Sophie tried to remember what she'd had for breakfast—afraid for a second, until she remembered the bowl of cereal. Lunch wasn't for another hour, at the Valley Diner with Tory Sanders. Someone who knew about her past struggle—and would soon know about her relapse. Someone who would make certain that she ate enough, but not too much. Someone who would follow her to the bathroom if need be.

And report to Phyllis.

Sophie was on course.

"So what's this really about?" Matt's question brought her back to the present.

"It appears I'm not real fond of myself again."

"The bulimia's back."

"Yep."

"Do you know why?"

"I'm guessing it has to do with the fact that Duane's going to be running for state office."

"And?"

"I'm not good for his image." Nor did she want to face the press. Or change the life she and Duane had. Or…

"Because of your age." Didn't take him long to see the problem.

"And because I exude."

"Exude? What does that mean?"

"I make men think naughty thoughts."

His bark of laughter shocked her. "Ah, hon, men have been thinking naughty thoughts since the dawn of time. Way before your advent into the world."

"But I bring them out in men."

Matt was quiet for a long moment. "Maybe," he finally admitted, his expression serious. "But not from anything you do or say. You're an unusual woman, Soph. You've got looks that stop guys in their tracks, no doubt about that. But you've also got this warmth about you, a look in your eye, that any man would be a fool to pass up."

"You did."

"Because a good man doesn't take what he can't return. I wasn't in love with you."

"Duane says he love me."

"Then he probably does. He's not the sort to lie. Especially about something like that."

She agreed.

"And what's more, I believe in you." Matt's words startled her further.

"What does that mean?"

"A good woman doesn't give just because a man is foolish enough to want," he said. "She gives when her heart is involved. That's a lesson most girls learn from their mothers, but you learned it the hard way. And I think you feel it more deeply than anyone I've ever met."

She might buy that, if not for the sheer number of her former lovers.

"I think that's why you beat yourself up so badly over the past. Because you were not only learning a lesson the hard way, but you were hurting the very thing you were trying to serve—your heart."

He must really like her to be so blind to the whorishness of those years.

"Tell me this, Sophie. When you made those choices—"

"Spread my legs for anyone who'd have me, you mean."

Nothing but the truth was going to work here. Those weren't just college boys, college romances, they were talking about.

"Slept with more guys than you'd have liked," he countered, "was there ever a time when you had sex for money?"

"Of course not."

"Did you allow your stepfather to continue to touch you inappropriately after that first time or two, when you were too scared to know what to do?"

Matt knew she hadn't. She'd known that to tell her mother would have done no good, but she'd made damn certain she wasn't alone with the man even for a second after that. Had never been in the house with him without her mother there. Had kept herself either in her mother's presence or behind a locked door.

And had been lucky that he'd been on his way out of her mother's life, anyway.

"Was there ever a time you entered into a liaison thinking it was only for sex?"

She tried to remember.

"Or did you let those men take you into their arms because you'd hoped to find love and acceptance there? If not permanently, then at least for a time? You slept with them because you wanted your heart to be involved with them. You wanted them to care about you."

She shrugged. "That's every girl's fantasy, isn't it?"

"Every *good* girl's fantasy."

But Sophie knew that good girls didn't say yes as many times as she had. And she feared that, in spite of her changed life, if she let go of the way she'd organized her life, carefully maintaining control of all she could control— if she risked everything by letting Duane in further, by going to Phoenix, and lost—she'd be right back where she'd been before: looking for love in all the wrong places.

And hating herself.

After all, old habits died hard.

CHAPTER TWELVE

ONCE A WEEK Duane met Allen Newsome for "lunch" on the racquetball court, where they served up little rubber balls, attempting to cram them down each other's throats. The practice left their digestive systems without much to do, but over the more than twenty years they'd been partaking of the delicacy, Duane had grown stronger, healthier.

He'd also grown to respect the opinion of the man he'd met in law school. Like Duane, Allen had married young. Unlike Duane, Allen was still married to the same woman. Two of the Newsome kids were married. The youngest was in college.

All this time and Allen could still serve up one hell of a swing.

"That's game," Duane panted after a particularly challenging rally, tossing his friend the little black ball. "Your serve."

The beginning of game two. Duane was up one. Barely. Fifteen-fourteen—a good match. But he could win. He could do this.

Sleep deprived or not.

Game two went to Allen. By two points.

And because he'd accumulated the most points, Allen had the first serve in game three. The balding, still-slim man stood in the back corner of the small, wooden walled room, his racquet in one hand and the ball in the other. He glanced at Duane.

"I saw you at Charles's Place yesterday."

His lunch date with Sophie.

"Why didn't you say something?" he asked, waiting for the serve. Guys didn't regularly stand around and chat during a competitive racquetball match.

As a general rule, he and Allen never did. A practice he'd like to continue.

"I was with clients." Allen, a partner in a private securities firm, seemed to do a lot of business over lunch. But then, he was the rainmaker. Always had been.

"You going to serve that thing?"

"I just…" Allen raised the ball, then dropped his hand again. "Who is she?"

"Her name's Sophie."

"Does she…I mean, would she be interested in, you know, meeting anyone else?"

He didn't just say that. The bastard didn't just say that. "Meeting?" The squeeze Duane gave to the strings of his racquet should have broken them. "As in how?"

"I don't know." Allen's grin was almost shy. It made Duane sick. "Just for lunch. Maybe."

That *maybe* reverberated through the room, and through Duane's entire being.

"I thought you and Sandy were solid," he said, trying to see through the red haze clouding his vision. To hold on and not kill the man who was only a few short feet away.

"We are. It's just…we're forty-six, man. Life's passing by too quickly. And besides, why should you have all the fun? What, you don't want to share a little?"

He was going to kill him. If Duane didn't get out of that room, immediately, he was going to kill the man.

How Duane managed to walk calmly to the door, he couldn't say. How he opened it without pulling it off its hinges, he'd never know. With one foot on the floor outside the court he turned back.

"Sophie's my fiancée." He didn't manage to temper the biting anger in his voice. "If you ever get within five hundred feet of her, I will kill you with my own hands."

In the space of two minutes and two questions, a relationship that had spanned decades ended.

AT THIRTY-FIVE, Tory Sanders still carried a bit of the fragile-waif look she'd had when Sophie first met her, eight years before. Today the appearance came more from the textured, short dark hair with bangs that hung over Tory's big blue eyes than it did from the circumstances of her life.

"I'm not totally buying it, you know," she said, chewing a bite of the Cobb salad she'd ordered—the same thing she always ordered—as she sat across from Sophie.

Becca Parsons was at the diner, a few tables over, having lunch with her three sisters and their weird little mother, who was as vintage in dress as she was in age. Rose didn't get out much anymore, but Becca always made certain her mom attended their once-a-week girls' lunch.

"You're eating fine," Tory continued.

"Because I'm consciously making myself do so."

"Or because you're hungry. Last time, when you were aware of the disorder and working on it, you'd eat, but you'd stare at every bite first, like you had to make friends with it, make your peace with it before you could put it in your mouth."

"I did?"

Tory nodded.

"No one else ever told me that."

"Maybe because they didn't notice. They all knew you, Soph. They probably had to make peace with every bite, too, in their own way. But you and I had just met. I was an outsider, observing the facts. Taking it in. Truth be known—" Tory leaned in farther "—I was watching so closely because I was half-afraid I was suffering from some kind of disorder myself."

"But you looked great! You'd just had Chrissie and seemed so together and happy."

"I was happy. Crazily so. And scared as hell to believe it would last."

Scared to believe because she'd known the dark side of love with an abusive and maniacal husband. Sophie knew the story, mostly from Phyllis, whose best friend, Christine, had been Tory's older sister. Christine was dead—murdered by Tory's ex while Sophie had still been in college.

"Anyway," Tory said, ending a long moment of silence, "after Chrissie was born I went through this whole head-trip thing where Ben wouldn't love me anymore because I was fat. Which was crazy, of course, but I was so busy being afraid that I did all kinds of things to sabotage us."

Sophie took another bite of protein-loaded tuna. "Like what?"

"Anytime Ben told me he loved me, I'd tell myself he really didn't. That he didn't know me well enough yet."

Sophie quit chewing.

"As badly as I wanted to cuddle up to him at night, I'd lie

there stiffly on my side of the bed, waiting for him to come to me, because I was afraid he didn't want me touching him."

"Did he reach for you?"

"For a time. Until he started to think that I'd changed my mind about him. See, that's the dangerous thing about doubts. They backfire on you. Ben loves me as much as I love him. But the more I feared his lack of love, the more I withdrew, and the more I withdrew, the more I convinced him that I didn't love him, when the truth was I love him more and more every day. Even now."

Was Sophie doing that? Sabotaging her relationship with Duane? Or were their problems completely different?

"He knows that now, though, right?"

"Yeah." Tory's eyes grew shadowed. "But I still have hard days, times when the memories bring back feelings of being worth less than everyone else. If I don't recognize it happening, I start to withdraw. I get these horrible feelings of aloneness."

Sophie related so much to the things Tory was saying that it scared her. As did the prognosis.

"Even after all these years?" She didn't really want to hear the answer.

"Yeah. But there's a difference."

"And that is?"

"Ben gets it now. When I start to withdraw, he sticks to me like glue, making certain that I know how much he loves me."

Would Sophie ever have that with Duane? Did she want it?

All of her instincts screamed out against knocking down the wall of privacy that kept her safe—especially now, when she needed all of her inner resources up and working. This was a time to pull in. To survive. Not a time to experiment.

Yet she'd taken Duane's key.

"I've been seeing Duane Koch," she blurted.

"Yeah."

"What do you mean, *yeah?*"

"Sophie, this is Shelter Valley. What part of living in a small town did you miss? Do you think there was a single one of us who didn't know the first time Will's friend's car was parked outside your home all night?"

They hadn't hidden the car. But Sophie's house was outside of town.

"No one said anything."

"We're nosy and we care," Tory said. "We aren't insensitive."

Sophie's stomach dropped and she wished she hadn't eaten three-quarters of a sandwich that might very well be revisiting her.

"Everyone knows I've been sleeping with him for almost two years."

"Well, no one actually discusses your sex life, for heaven's sake. You're an adult, Soph. And most of us have had sex outside of marriage. People just don't want to see you get hurt."

"And the general consensus is that he'll hurt me?"

Tory shrugged. "I haven't heard a general consensus. You guys have some challenges, to be sure, but then so did most of the rest of us. Look at Martha. She was an atheist with four kids when she and the Preach met."

A divorced atheist. Her husband—a college professor at Montford—had left her for one of his students. A woman half his age.

He'd been a friend of Will's, too.

The same age as Duane.

Everyone had called it a midlife crisis.

Fear prickled the back of Sophie's neck.

"So back to the bulimia," Tory said to Sophie after Nancy, the diner's hostess and general all-around jump-in-and-help person, had cleared their plates. "I really don't think you need to worry so much about it. I saw you then, and there's no resemblance to the you I see now."

"I almost threw up twenty minutes ago," Sophie told her.

"But it's only been happening since Saturday night, right?"

"That's the first time I actually got sick."

"And the fasting—you've always done that when you're on the job. I remember when we all worked on the summer theater program a couple of years ago. You'd get so caught up in creating your magic, you'd lose track of time."

"I gorged myself last night." She wasn't going to hide this time, even if Tory, bless her soul, wanted to try to lighten her load. "And I purged."

Tory's eyes narrowed. "You weren't just sick?"

Shaking her head, Sophie told her how she'd fought the nausea, the urge to lose her dinner, then had given in to it.

"I'm still not convinced." Tory couldn't seem to let it go. "You were feeling nausea before you stuck your finger in your throat."

"Yes, but—"

"I don't know, Soph. I'm telling you, you don't look at all like you did before. Your eyes are clear. You don't have the guilt lines around your mouth every time you glance at food. Your skin color's good."

"Well, I sure don't have the flu."

"So…maybe you're pregnant."

Sophie shook her head. "Duane and I use condoms." She repeated out loud what she'd told herself at two o'clock that morning, when she'd lain awake alone in her bed and panicked at the thought that she could be unwed and pregnant. With the child of a man who probably wasn't right for her. But there was no reason to fear that nightmare. None.

Sex for her had always included condoms. Every single time. In the olden days, she'd carried them in her purse. And she'd never been pregnant. Or had any sexually related problems, either.

"Condoms are only ninety-eight percent safe."

"I'm not pregnant," Sophie repeated, refusing to give in to the unfounded fear again. She had enough to worry about.

"Well, I am."

JUST BECAUSE TORY was pregnant didn't mean Sophie was. She worked hard that afternoon—designed a set, played with various lighting opportunities. She cleaned out the refrigerator and turned on the self-cleaning oven.

Then she threw up again.

Sitting with her back against the bathroom door, a cool washcloth against her cheeks, she stared at the whitewashed cupboards she'd loved so much when she'd first seen them.

They were bright and homey at the same time.

A new world, and a sense of security all wrapped up in a piece of wood with a little brass knob.

She wasn't pregnant.

Even with a violent bout of vomiting behind her, the words still rang true to Sophie. She wasn't pregnant. She was bulimic.

It always happened this way. She'd put all of her sights on a man, and when things got rough, take it out on herself. She'd panic. Remember her mother.

And know that she was her mother's daughter.

But all of her sights weren't on Duane. She very carefully hadn't allowed that to happen.

She'd bought this home on her own, with money she'd made from her successful career. She had a home. Security.

She had friends who were as close as family. Better, in fact, than the family she'd been born into.

And she'd brought Duane to her home not because of what he might offer her, not because she was afraid and needed to be taken care of, but because she'd been drawn to him. Physically attracted, certainly, but emotionally and intellectually attracted even more.

In the beginning, being with him seemed to make life that much more vibrant. Like there'd been something she'd been missing and found. Something she hadn't even known to yearn for.

It still felt that way when she could relax and be with him. She didn't regret bringing Duane home. Didn't think any less of herself for getting involved with him. Even if their relationship didn't work out, she'd entered into it for the right reasons.

Her past was what was killing them—and bringing on the bulimic relapse. It made sense. That old lifestyle had brought on the disorder to begin with. And now that those old choices were rising to haunt her, so was the bulimia. Her past blighted her current reputation. And gave birth to Duane's jealousy, too.

Her past was fact. A part of her. She couldn't make it go away.

That meant she couldn't take the same risks as others; she had to keep a closer watch on her emotional health because it directly affected her physical well-being.

She couldn't afford a media blitz. And she wasn't sure

she could afford to be all-in with one person, either. She'd become too dependent—start to get her self-worth from him. And if he ever left her, where would that leave her? If Duane decided the price of being with her was too high, and chose his career instead, what would happen to her?

Yeah, that's where the bulimia was coming from.

Sophie stared at her hands, at the scratch mark from a lighting incident earlier that afternoon.

Not one person she knew in the entertainment industry would blink at anything the press had to say about her. She was the tame one, the responsible one, in that world.

She owned more of her home than the bank did. And would still own it, be able to pay for it, love it, if she never saw Duane Koch again.

So why the bulimia?

Because she couldn't bear to be responsible for ruining her lover's career and lifelong aspirations?

Opening her mind to the things Phyllis had said about the disorder, Sophie looked for answers that were eluding her. She'd talked to the people closest to her. And they'd told her a lot of different things.

"Every *good* girl's fantasy." Matt's words. He thought she was nurturing. So caring that he'd been tempted to have a relationship with her.

"We know that the basis of your eating troubles stems from the way you view yourself." Phyllis.

"So…maybe you're pregnant." Tory.

"Duane and I use condoms." Her.

"Condoms are only ninety-eight percent safe." Tory again.

"I'm not pregnant." Sophie said the words aloud to convey how much she meant them. How much she believed them.

Or at least, how much she wanted to believe them.

Had to believe them.

Her stomach started to curdle again.

"Oh God," she said as she leaned over the bowl once more.

Ten minutes later she was on her way to a convenience store out by the casino—one where not a single soul would know or care who she was or what she was about.

And forty-five minutes later, back at home, looking at the tiny little stick, she swore.

So much for ninety-eight percent effective.

CHAPTER THIRTEEN

DUANE WAS STILL FUMING over his lunchtime experience as he drove to Shelter Valley after work that evening. His Mercedes quietly hummed along, putting miles between him and Phoenix, and, eventually, allowing a sense of peace to filter in.

Somehow he was going to have to convince Sophie to marry him. And convince himself that it was right to marry her. That was the only way this was going to work. Other men needed to know she was taken. Period.

The men he'd be introducing her to needed to know she was his woman. Exclusively. That she had his protection.

And deserved their respect.

Almost wishing he'd brought the ring with him, Duane pulled to a stop in front of her house, looking at the place anew—as his second home as well as hers. The palm tree needed to be trimmed of its dead fronds.

And maybe they should add some bougainvillea. If she wanted to, of course. If she agreed to marry him. If they really followed through on the idea.

He reached the front door and lifted his hand to knock. Then used his key instead. He was more than Sophie's friend. Or sleeping buddy. He wasn't a mere visitor in her life.

Was he?

She'd asked him many times to use his key.

He should have done so. Maybe, if he'd acted more like a partner than a lover, she wouldn't be doubting the sincerity and depth of his affections so much.

And maybe he wouldn't be, either.

"Soph?"

Was there no end to the ways he'd done her wrong? Shortchanged her?

Would a lifetime of tending to her be enough?

She wasn't in the living room. Or the kitchen. "Soph?"

Could he be there for her? Be enough for her? Trust her enough not to destroy her with his jealousy? Interest her enough to keep her attention?

She wasn't in the bedroom, either. But from the window, he saw her in the backyard. Talking to a man who had to be standing on a ladder on the other side of the wall.

He was picking oranges, if the scooped, long-handled tool in his hand was anything to judge by. Unless, of course, he simply wanted it to look like he was harvesting fruit off the laden tree in his backyard, as an excuse to spy on his neighbor, get her attention.

When Sophie wasn't out of town she worked from the home office in what used to be the second bedroom. All day, every day.

And based on what she'd said about the winter visitor, James Benson was around all day, too.

Stomach churning, Duane stood watching them. And the more he stared, the hotter he got.

He shoved his hands into his pockets. *Cool it, man.*

The voice of reason wasn't very loud.

She knows you're on your way. She wouldn't be having

a liaison right under your nose. She wouldn't have a liaison, period. If Sophie was going to turn to another man, she'd break things off with you first.

But then, isn't that exactly what she'd intended to do at lunch?

He was in Shelter Valley half an hour earlier than she'd expected. Maybe he should leave and come back. See if she was in the house alone. See if she mentioned her visit with her neighbor.

Hell no, she wouldn't mention it. You made such an ass of yourself the last time the man's name came up she wouldn't dare trust you with it again.

She smiled. Nodded. Didn't seem to be in any hurry to end the conversation.

Duane had asked her to end her friendship with the man. And here she was, less than forty-eight hours later, having a conversation with him. At home. So what if Duane had been out of line? If she loved him, wouldn't she respect him, issues and all? Wouldn't she understand that he meant no harm?

Wouldn't she love him enough to give up talking with a virtual stranger because her continuing to do so added to their already overwhelming struggles? Unless the stranger meant something to her, too.

In a sense she was choosing him over Duane. Choosing her conversations with him over Duane's needs.

In a sense, you're driving yourself crazy, man.

In a sense, she doesn't deserve this.

In a sense, you should get your ass out there and act like the man she deserves you to be. The partner she deserves you to be. The man you know, deep down, you are.

Believe in her.

Trust her.

It wasn't Sophie he doubted. Not really. Not so much. It was the men who looked at her.

A likeness of Allen's face swam in his mind's eye—the bashfulness, the anticipation.

And Duane knew he had more work to do before he could trust himself to behave appropriately when other men were around Sophie.

He wasn't ready to marry her yet.

SOPHIE WAS IN THE KITCHEN, adding fresh diced tomatoes and red onions to the Alfredo pasta she'd prepared for dinner, when Duane arrived. She wasn't panicking. Wasn't telling anyone anything. She was going on with life as usual. For today.

She had time—months—before anything happened.

Other than making a doctor's appointment, there was nothing else about today's information that needed her immediate attention.

She could go on.

She had time.

Duane didn't have to know tonight. She was still too stunned by her news to know how to break it to him.

She needed a plan first. A solid idea of what she thought she should do with the rest of her life, before she allowed him any say in the situation.

She had time.

She also had a baby growing in her belly.

She had time.

Up to nine months.

Then she'd have a baby in her life.

Duane used his key instead of knocking, and Sophie's

smile as she greeted him was meant to look completely natural.

She was fine.

She had time.

"HEY, COME TAKE A LOOK at this." Sophie darted down the hall after they finished washing the dishes—after a dinner that she ate well, with only a little prodding on his part. She pulled Duane toward her office and workshop as though she couldn't get there fast enough.

Or couldn't slow down enough to actually look at him.

Or have any real conversation.

She'd been that way ever since he'd arrived. As though she had a secret she couldn't tell him.

And Duane, with a growing sense of doom, knew what she was hiding.

Her friendship with her new neighbor. She wasn't going to end it.

Or tell him about their conversation that afternoon.

Duane didn't know what he was going to do about that.

She'd been toying with different scrims all afternoon, she told him as they walked, attempting to layer them in such a way that with a combination of special lighting techniques, she could create a three-dimensional forest with a horse running through it for a show she was doing in April. She wanted his opinion on the end result.

They were in crisis and all she wanted to talk about was fantasy? Because that's all they'd ever really been—a great fantasy? Created right there in her home. Maintained there.

Unable to emerge in the real world?

The forest was scaled down, of course, enough to fit on the four-foot-by-six-foot stage built along one side of the room. He knew from previous visits to what he'd dubbed her "magical kingdom" that the various lights, from the ellipsoidals to the Fresnels—and the curtains—scrims, cycs and others—were completely true in form, content and action to what he'd find on a full-size stage. Even the rigging was authentic, with all working parts. The previous year for Christmas she'd installed a custom intelligent lighting system.

Basically, anything Sophie did on someone else's stage, she tried at home first.

He watched as she adjusted, flipped switches and, piece by piece, turned half the room into a forest. He even stepped back when the horse came galloping toward him. Any other time he'd have been awed at her ability. Tonight he wondered if maybe they were facing the beginning of their end.

"It works, huh?" Sophie asked, watching his reaction with complete focus.

"It's amazing, babe." He used his old nickname for her. And wondered why he was still there at all.

He didn't think there was anything sexual between Sophie and James. At least not yet.

But one thing was for certain—the man's presence had created a wedge between Duane and Sophie that was only getting bigger.

Or was Duane doing that?

Maybe he should come clean about his early arrival that evening.

But his illogical insecurity where she was concerned wasn't her problem. It was his. And he wasn't going to let it spill over onto her again. He didn't want her to see it. Not now. Not when she was already pulling away from him.

He missed her. Their time together in her home had always seemed so perfect.

Until recently.

Now all of his time with her seemed rife with problems. Issues were stacking up against them more quickly than he could decipher them.

Duane wondered again if it was time to let her go.

CHAPTER FOURTEEN

SOPHIE NEEDED TO FEEL Duane moving inside her. Needed him connected to her in the most consuming way. And apparently he needed the communion as badly as she did.

By eight o'clock that night, without having had any personal conversation at all, they were naked in her bed, their bodies moving in a familiar rhythm, and yet moving differently, as well. Duane seemed to caress more deeply, to reach further as he took them both to a physical ecstasy that obliterated the world.

Until nothing mattered but floating together on the powerful waves.

As she lay with him afterward, Sophie came back to reality with a crash. Duane was forty-six years old.

He'd be sixty-four—old enough to receive social security—by the time her baby graduated from high school.

She had to tell him.

But not yet. Not until she had that plan. Not until she knew that she wasn't going to expect him to calm her panic. To provide her and her baby with security.

Not until she knew she wouldn't let this latest challenge send her right back to a loss of self. To becoming a dependent little twit again, believing she had to have a man to take care of her, to be safe.

"Tory's pregnant," she blurted, in lieu of bringing up the pregnancy she so desperately needed to announce.

"Tory and Ben, right?" He didn't sound all that sleepy. Or lethargic, either.

"Right." They'd been at Becca and Will's for a Christmas party that Duane and Sophie had attended—separately.

"How old is Tory now?"

"Thirty-five."

"Is she happy about the baby?" He shifted, but didn't pull her closer. He lay, instead, on his back, one arm under his head.

"She's ecstatic. Ben is, too, apparently. I guess they originally wanted six kids."

Duane didn't say anything.

Sophie tensed. "One seems like a lot to keep up with to me," she ventured.

She had to tell him.

But not like this.

"Mmm-hmm."

Oh, God, what am I going to do?

Duane rolled over, landing half on top of her as he slid his engorged penis along her thigh and up toward her groin.

He was going to make love to her again.

And she was going to let him.

A MESSAGE FROM THE CHAIRPERSON of the Maricopa County branch of his party awaited Duane at his office the next morning. He needed Duane to return his call as soon as possible.

Rubbing eyes heavy from lack of sleep, Duane poured a cup of coffee, preparing to fill his calendar with dates for the rest of the spring and summer. And fall, too.

That was the life of a candidate. Campaigning. Serving. Making himself available.

A small thrill of anticipation accompanied the thought.

This was what he was made for. What he was good at. What he enjoyed.

And so it began….

"COOL. Sophie, what'd you say this thing's called?" Calvin tossed the beanbag across several feet of desert landscaping in Sophie's backyard toward the plastic ramp, aiming for the hole in the center.

"Cornhole. Some guys were playing it in the hallway backstage at the last show I was at, and it looked like fun."

Kids had a way of making life feel okay. Even when it was never going to be the same again.

"What'd you bring me?" Clarissa was a princess today in her braids, pink T-shirt dress and stretch pants.

"Rissa, that's rude," Calvin said, tossing another bag.

"I know, but Sophie doesn't care. Do you, Soph?"

Sophie tugged the little girl's braid, wondering if she was going to have a girl. "Not really, especially since I told you Monday that I brought you something. But your mom would care if she heard you, and if anyone else did they'd say you weren't nice, so let's refrain, huh?"

"'Kay." Clarissa nodded, the serious look back on her face. "This is boring. Can we color, please?"

When Duane had called Wednesday morning to tell her that he had a political dinner meeting that night, she'd immediately phoned Phyllis with a request to have the twins over. And was happy she had.

She'd been glad to have the break from Duane, too.

"Coloring's for sissies." Calvin ran to collect the eight bags he'd thrown. "C'mon, let's play this."

"I'll tell you what," Sophie said, having more trouble than usual mediating between the twins that afternoon. "We'll all three play one game of cornhole. Then while Calvin practices, you and I'll go inside and see what I brought you, Clarissa."

"How come I have to practice?" Calvin asked, a bag suspended in midair. "I want to see what Rissa got."

"You need to practice because you want to be able to beat your dad when he plays with you, right?" Calvin was always trying to be as good as Matt, who let him be only often enough to keep up the boy's confidence, without giving him unrealistic expectations of himself or others. And Sophie was always trying to be half as good with the twins as their parents were.

How in hell was she ever going to raise a child of her own?

"But you can still see what I brought for your sister. Since when do we keep secrets from each other?" she added as Calvin went back to throwing.

"I know a secret." Clarissa's hand slid into hers as the little girl gazed at her with a curious sadness in her eyes.

"What's that?"

"Somebody doesn't want you around her husband."

"What?" Bending down, Sophie held both of Clarissa's hands as she met the little girl eye to eye. "Who?"

"I dunno."

"Why?"

"'Cause you're pretty. Gorgeous." She said the word slowly, as though having a hard time getting her tongue around it.

"Who told you that?"

"No one. I heard Mommy and Daddy talking."

Sophie could hear the beanbags landing. Was aware of

the sound of Calvin's tennis shoes against the rocks as he retrieved and threw again. Could even make out the "All rights" and disappointed "Ohs" he emitted.

But there was no sunshine. No blue skies. Or fruit trees. No life.

JUST FIVE MINUTES EARLY, Duane was surprised to find he was the only party member present at the downtown Phoenix steak house that offered, in addition to great food, secluded table settings where sensitive business could be discussed in relative privacy. Wendt's used to be a gentlemen-only establishment and still largely catered to men.

Michael Burke, chairperson for the past two years, had set the meeting for six.

Duane gave his name and was shown immediately to a booth in the back of the smallest room, next to an unlit stone fireplace.

A booth that wouldn't fit more than four people. Apparently tonight's planning session was going to be intimate.

Which was the way he liked it. More could be said, more could be accomplished, if there weren't so many interests involved.

The place was rapidly filling, mostly with professional men.

Seeing himself as one of a crowd, maybe a crowd that Sophie would consider boring and stuffy, Duane looked around. With a quick glance, he recognized a judge at one table, a congressman at another. All having the requisite cocktail. Ordering steak. The rituals part of running their small portions of the world.

So were they all really making a difference in those

portions, or were they simply a bunch of penguins suffering from pluralistic ignorance?

He couldn't speak for the rest of them, but he was there to make a difference.

He waved at Michael as the older man entered and walked toward him. In his day job the tall, gray-haired man was superintendent of schools for one of the local districts.

"Who else is joining us?" Duane asked as Michael slid onto the bench opposite.

"No one." He waved for their waiter. "What would you like to drink?" he asked Duane, ordering a scotch and water for himself.

"I'll have the same."

"I don't have a lot of time." Michael folded his hands on the table between them. "I've got a school board meeting at seven-thirty."

It was six. And Michael worked twenty minutes from downtown. Twenty minutes in good traffic.

He asked if Duane had been in the court. Then how his day in the office had been, basically keeping the conversation on small talk until their drinks arrived and they ordered dinner.

Michael had taken out no folders, no writing pads, no PDA or sheets of paper. Clearly, Duane had misunderstood the reason for this meeting. Clearly something was wrong.

"What's up?" he asked. If they'd changed their mind about his nomination, he'd run on his own. That quick decision settled something inside Duane.

A loyal party member for all of his adult life, he didn't relish the idea of running as an independent, but he'd do it. He belonged at the state level.

He could make a difference.

Being a lawmaker, a mover in this world, was his

destiny. Sitting here, waiting for Michael to speak, Duane finally realized how much the opportunity meant to him.

And, as Michael sat silently for a tense moment, Duane wondered if Will Parsons knew about this meeting.

Will would've called, Duane told himself.

"My wife's book club met at Charles's Place for lunch on Monday."

Rapidly switching mental gears, Duane pushed his drink to the side. Were Allen Newsome and Michael Burke somehow connected? "If this is going where I think it is, we're through here," he said, needing to leave before he irrevocably closed a door he didn't want to shut.

He'd lost a friendship this week. He didn't intend to lose a party, too.

"I think you'll want to listen, Duane," Burke said. "We've known each other for years, labored side by side at various precincts long into the night on numerous occasions, celebrated victories and commiserated through defeats. That at least gives me enough standing with you to deserve a chance to say my piece."

Eyes narrowed, Duane acknowledged the claim with a nod. Michael's assertions were true, and they didn't sound anything like Allen's approach the day before.

"I think you know how hard I've been working for this nomination for you," Michael said. "Not only within our ranks, but outside, as well. I already have hundreds of nonparty votes ready to be cast for you."

"I appreciate that."

"I'm behind you because I believe you are, by far, the best man for this job. Like the rest of the nation, Arizona's been in crisis. Economy notwithstanding, we have the whole border-control challenges to face."

With solutions they agreed upon.

"This state needs you, Duane. It needs your intelligence. And it needs your integrity."

"It has it."

"I'm not doubting that. What I'm doubting is your ability to get elected if you suddenly become someone we don't recognize."

Surely Michael wasn't insinuating that Duane's run for office meant he had to live alone and celibate for the rest of his life. That was ludicrous. Garbage. It was a well-known fact that a spouse and family often helped a candidate get elected.

Of course, they weren't talking about a traditional-looking family. They were talking about Sophie. A woman who looked more like his daughter than his wife.

"I'm not begrudging you a personal life, Duane. Nor am I standing in judgment. If you want to entertain ten young women at once, you have my blessing. But please, I'm urging—even begging—you to do so discreetly."

"You just said the state needs my integrity, but you want me to hide my personal life?"

"Not your life, man, just the young things. We talk about family values and a return to the mores of a cleaner, more successful America. We aren't going to be able to sell a man who squires young blondes around town."

Young blondes. Duane's mind reeled. He'd expected opposition, but not nearly so blatantly. And not so quickly, either. "She could have been a client. Did you think of that?"

Weak, man. And defensive—as though you're guilty of something. You're going to have to do far better than that if you ever hope to pull off having it all.

"Not by the way you were looking at her, according to Suzanne."

Damn Suzanne Burke and her book club. They could dictate his right to choose his lovers?

Peering at a man he trusted, Duane made a decision. "She's not a fling, Michael," he said, in spite of the distant goodbye he and Sophie had given each other this morning. The closemouthed kiss. "I've been seeing her for more than two years. I've asked her to marry me."

Now didn't seem like a good time to admit that Sophie had refused.

Or maybe it was. He could tell Michael not to worry, that he and Sophie were having problems. He could end this meeting on a good note, right now. Enjoy his newly arrived steak, some invigorating political strategy conversation, a drink or two, then go home to a good night's rest.

Rather than looking relieved at the news of Duane's marriage proposal, Michael was frowning. His heavy sigh was not encouraging. Nor was the slow shake of his head.

"The timing's not good, Duane. Surely you can see that."

Duane could. So why wasn't he walking away from Sophie? Right now?

"How about if I marry her immediately, quietly, then we present her as my wife, as though she'd been around for a while?" he asked, just to hedge his bets. To find out how problematic the situation might actually be.

"How many people do you know in this town?"

"Hundreds."

"And how many of them have you socialized with over the past two years?"

"A hundred. At least."

"How many of them have met this girl?"

"None." Duane held up his hand before Michael made his point any more clear. Sophie's presence was going to cause a sensation, no matter what role she played. "Men fall in love. They marry."

"Generally with women of their own generation," Michael said. "Don't get me wrong, you've been alone a long time and no one will be happier than I am to know that you've finally found someone to share your life. But the public's not going to see happily-ever-after. They're going to see scandal. Trust me, this gets out and you'll be a sugar daddy by the morning's paper. And you know where that leads?" Michael didn't wait for an answer. "They start to think if you don't have the sense to see that this girl's using you, then you aren't going to be savvy enough to see through all the users in the state, either."

"Sophie doesn't need my money. She's got plenty of her own. She runs a company. Is sought after in her field all over the nation." Why in the hell was he defending her so adamantly? He'd just realized what this political position meant to him.

It was time to let Sophie go.

"What is her field?" Michael asked, as though searching for a crumb he could use to bake something people would eat.

"Theater production." Duane could elaborate, talk about Sophie's talent with lighting and special effects, but the look on Michael's face said there was no point.

"She's an artist."

"Of sorts. Yes."

"Theater people don't carry the image of conservatism."

Duane wanted to argue that, but he couldn't. Mostly because, though he had yet to admit it to himself, he shared Michael's view.

"So if she's not after your money, the next slant will be that you're experiencing a midlife crisis. Running around with a girl young enough to be your daughter. People will be afraid to trust the judgment of a man who can't see what a fool he's making of himself."

"Don't you think you're making a bit much of this?"

"Do you? Honestly?"

Taking time to come up with the best answer, the reply that would put an end to this craziness, Duane cut his steak. Took a bite. Then another.

"Tell me this," Michael said, in between bites of his own. "If you weren't a little bit worried about this Sophie's public reception, why have you been keeping her a secret for two years? Why am I, a man you associate with on a regular basis, only now hearing that you have a girlfriend, let alone have met a woman you intend to marry?"

Duane hadn't actually said he intended to marry her. Only that he'd asked.

He placed his silverware carefully along the edge of his plate. "I love her, Michael."

Apparently this was a night for hard truths. Personal truths.

"So wait until after November. Until after you're elected."

The idea was tempting. Putting the whole Sophie crisis off was tempting. If she'd hang around while he went on with his life.

He tried to come up with an explanation for his constituents as to why he'd kept his young love hidden long enough to get their vote. No matter what words he'd use to spin things, his actions would be saying exactly what he'd inadvertently been saying for two years: he was ashamed of Sophie, of his liaison with her. There was something wrong in their being together. They had something to hide. She wasn't good enough for him. They didn't belong together in real life.

He couldn't do that to her. Especially not with the onset of bulimia. He wasn't stupid. He knew his choices were partially to blame for the relapse of his lover's confidence issues.

If he had to keep her hidden, he had to set her free.

"Wait until after November?" he asked. "Where's the integrity in that suggestion?"

Michael drained his glass.

"I don't know," he finally said, wiping his mouth and laying his napkin on top of his plate. "I just know that if you insist on pursuing this…this relationship right now, and the polls start to reflect a negative impact, I might not be able to do anything to help you."

"Might not be able to, or won't?"

Michael's pause was painful, in a masculine, professional way. "I don't know," he said again, standing.

Duane stood, too, picking up the check. "Then I guess I have to take my chances," he said, not sure why he was fighting for something that was probably ending anyway— especially when he was absolutely certain he wanted Michael's support. "You go ahead, I'll take care of this."

With a handshake and a seeming attempt to return their relationship to the solid footing it had been on for many years, Michael told Duane he'd do what he could to counter any negative talk.

Duane thanked him. Paid the bill. Then drove home.

He didn't call Sophie to let her know that his meeting had ended far earlier than he'd expected.

He didn't invite her to drive to Phoenix for the night.

And didn't grab a suit and drive to Shelter Valley, either.

He stayed home and drank. The pressure was getting to him.

CHAPTER FIFTEEN

SOPHIE NEEDED HELP with the water pressure, and came up blank about who to call at one in the morning. She had been working on the site plan for Matt's show since early evening—minus the half hour she'd spent on the Internet, looking for an obstetrician in Tucson. There was absolutely no way she was going to the Shelter Valley clinic for this one.

And at eleven, she'd taken fifteen minutes to shower—more in need of the relaxing warm water running down her body than the cleansing.

As fate would have it, Duane had called during that quarter-hour time span to say good-night. He'd left a message, saying he was beat and going to bed.

He'd sounded odd, been vague about his campaign meeting, and she hadn't called him back.

She'd gone to work instead. For now she was anesthetized. Engrossed in the career she loved. Finding strength in the knowledge that she was good at what she did. That she could provide for herself.

And for a new person in her life, too.

She could provide, but couldn't get much further with her storm until she knew how many tubes she could install—the numbers would make a huge difference to lighting requirements and options. The number of tubular water drips depended on how much water pressure she could get to the stage.

A crib and a stage weren't both going to fit in this room.

Somebody doesn't want you around her husband. Clarissa's innocent words from earlier in the day slipped from the locked recesses of Sophie's mind.

For the sake of the little girl, who'd clearly been hurting on her behalf, Sophie had laughed all those hours ago. She'd tried to turn the overheard conversation into a joke. A compliment, even, that people thought Sophie was so lovely when, really, she burped a lot. She'd sucked in a lungful of air and emitted a somewhat loud offering to prove her point, and both kids had started giggling. There ensued a competition that had taken them completely away from any painful topics of conversation, until their mother had stopped on her way from the university to pick them up.

Sophie had turned on the television in her too-quiet house the second the Sheffields left, watched the Discovery Channel through a supper of crackers and peanut butter and bananas—grains, protein and fruit all in one. Then, with the stereo blaring an Eagles CD, she went to work.

Somebody doesn't want you around her husband.

The words had been terrible enough coming from Clarissa. But were they only a precursor to what was to come in the future? What about six or seven years from now? Would Sophie be hearing a rendition of those very same words from her own child?

No wonder Duane had wanted to keep her hidden away. True, she'd never asked to be included in his Phoenix life, never even asked to see inside his home, but he'd never offered, either. Because he was ashamed of her?

And what about now? How eager was he going to be to introduce his *pregnant* young girlfriend to his constituents?

She'd managed to finish preliminary quotes for a couple of projects. And to keep the evening's nourishment inside her body. And to decide that, in the morning, she was going to go see Phyllis for the second time that week.

Sophie hadn't come up with any plans. Not for her baby. Or for her and Duane. How could she tell him she was pregnant, with things the way they were between them? He'd feel forced to marry her—if for no other reason than to save face publicly. And one thing she knew for certain—a baby was no reason for two people to get married. Most particularly when they were on the verge of breaking up.

PHYLLIS WAS IN HER OFFICE—alone—during her one scheduled office hour Thursday morning. Dressed in a blue suit with a blue-and-white-striped blouse, she was the epitome of professionalism. Only the wild batch of red hair atop her head gave hint to the warmth within. That and the concerned look in her eyes when Sophie, wearing her usual theater attire of jeans and long-sleeved, button-up shirt, plopped into a seat in front of her.

"We have to talk," she said, needing this done. Perhaps all of life's problems—Duane, Clarissa's comment, the lack of self-confidence—were signs that it was time to move on. To leave Shelter Valley. To start a life of her own.

A new life where her baby would never know about her mother's past.

And her past life wasn't going to know about her baby?

Sophie was all grown-up now. Didn't need a family watching over her.

Giving her strength.

She was soon going to be the strength giver. In a new little family.

Phyllis moved a stack of papers to the side of her desk and folded her hands in front of her. "What's up?"

"I need to know what woman, or women, in Shelter Valley don't want me around their husbands."

A tilt of the head was Phyllis's only giveaway. "What are you talking about?"

"Hey, this is me," Sophie said, lack of sleep—and probably a good dose of hurt feelings, as well—making her less patient than she'd have liked. "Straight talk, remember?"

Phyllis's face remained placid for another few seconds, then her eyes and shoulders dropped at the same time. "Who told you?" she asked, glancing up.

Shrugging, Sophie said, "Doesn't matter. I need to know who's worried. And how widespread the sentiment is."

"As far as I know, it's only been said once. By one person."

So it was true. Not that Sophie had doubted Phyllis's precocious daughter. But Clarissa was only six. Remembering the game of telephone, how things were hilariously misconstrued in the retelling, Sophie had hoped…

"Who?"

"It doesn't matter, Soph. It meant nothing. Which is why I have no idea how or why you even heard about it."

"This is Shelter Valley," she reminded her friend dryly—a fact that was oft repeated, but generally as a reminder of the strength and comfort and sense of home and family that the community brought to them all. "And I need to know, Phyl. I was downtown this morning, running errands, and every time I saw someone I knew, I wondered if it was her. You say it's only one person, but right now, for me, it's every woman I know in this town."

Phyllis seemed at a loss for words.

"Is it Tory?" Maybe, because her friend was pregnant, she was feeling insecure about her looks. Tory had already admitted struggling with her self-image after she'd had Chrissie. From her, the words would be more understandable. Not quite so damaging.

"Of course not. And it's not like you think, Soph. This has nothing to do with you or your choices."

"My past, you mean."

"A past that's far worse in your own eyes than in anyone else's. When are you going to let it go? Forgive yourself?"

"How can I?" she asked, her voice too loud. "A woman not trusting me around her husband is a pretty clear reminder," she said, taking care to speak lower. "And look at Duane. He's admitted that he worries about my effect on his upcoming campaign."

And that was before she'd become a pregnant lover.

"I thought he was over that. You said yesterday that he gave you a key to his place."

"Yeah, and he didn't invite me to use it last night." She hadn't offered, either. "He's trying." That was true. "But that doesn't mean the problems have gone away. Only that we've chosen to face them."

Which was all a moot point now. The baby changed everything.

"It's all going to come out when the press finds out that he's seeing me. When he's seen with me."

"And that's as much a problem for you as it is for him, huh?"

Her friend had no idea. And Sophie couldn't give her one. Not yet. She was too raw. Too scared.

Too determined to get through this on her own, to prove

to herself, and to her unborn child, that she had what it took to be there for the two of them. That she was reliable.

That they could both count on her to come through for them.

Just as she'd been telling herself over and over through most of the long dark hours of the night.

She'd come through. She was not her mother.

"Of course the press is a problem for me," Sophie said. "I hate what I was." More now than ever. "I hate what I did."

"You were a kid with a skewed perception of relationships."

Yeah, tell that to her kid.

"I'd taken classes," Sophie said. "I knew society's general sense of right and wrong."

"In what circle?" Phyllis asked. "Right for a small, churchgoing community is completely different from right or even normal in San Francisco or New York."

Sophie had been raised in the Denver area.

"And if you watch television, which we know raised you, then the mores you lived by weren't all that bad. Heck, if you believe what you see on TV, there are teenagers taking drugs and having orgies after school, while their parents think they're at sports practice or studying with friends. Orgies, Soph. As in multiple partners in one day, not just in a lifetime."

"We both know that's extreme and that those kids, if they exist, are going to have a tough time ahead of them. If they even survive high school and make it to adulthood."

"But my point is, by growing up with only television for parental guidance—not to mention a mother whose example made extreme seem normal—you can be forgiven for looking for love in the wrong places."

"And just like the kids at those parties, my choices still follow me. They are a part of me."

"Only if you let them be. Yes, choices define your life, Soph, but you make new ones every single day. Life is a work in progress, and how we define it changes as we change, as our choices change. You know I was married before." Phyllis leaned forward, strength giving her voice a solid presence in the room. "His name was Brad. And for the time I was married to him, I was Brad's wife. But there's nothing about me that's Brad's now. I belong, fully and completely, to Matt. I'm Matt's wife. In every single sense of the word. Yes, I have a memory of that other choice, I certainly learned from it, but it absolutely does not define me."

Sophie, focused on every word, searched for the absolution Phyllis was attempting to help her find. Searched as much for the child just beginning to grow inside her as for herself.

"It could define me," Phyllis continued. "If I'd never opened myself up to love again, which was the choice I was living when I met Matt, I'd probably still be Brad's wife in my mind. And my definition of myself would be as Brad's ex-wife—still defined by the choice of having married the man.

"But I made a different choice, Soph."

"To marry Matt."

"To not see myself in terms of the choice I made to marry Brad. I had to learn to see me as a woman. A complete, three-dimensional person. To understand why I married Brad in the first place, to understand where the choice went wrong, and to move beyond it. To not let it drive the rest of my life. The man took four years. Maybe six. The rest are mine."

Could it really be so simple?

"So how do I choose to not be the girl that the press is going to dig up when my past comes to light?" Assuming she and Duane found a way beyond all of the obstacles.

"You hold your head high and you shine light on the most recent six years. You were a kid before that, Sophie. You're a monogamous, successful adult now."

"Uh-huh. And how am I going to get anyone to believe that, when people in my own town—at least one woman we know of—who's seen me live those six years, who's seen my choices, doesn't trust me around her own husband?"

Phyllis's silence instilled a bit of panic.

"What I know is that what you put out comes back at you." Sophie pressed home her point before the silence could drive her crazy. "Kind of like the Golden Rule the Preach is always spouting, you know? No one gets a free ride, Phyl. We all have to pay for our mistakes, one way or another."

"But every single guilty verdict comes with its own unique sentence, sweetie, based on the mitigating and aggravating facts of the crime. You weren't a whore, Soph, yet you continue to paint yourself as one. You punish yourself as though you were one. You were an abused and neglected young woman who just wanted what every single one of us wants. To love and be loved. You had a skewed perception of how to go about making that happen."

"I wasn't abused."

The expletive that burst from Phyllis shocked Sophie—not because she hadn't heard it before, but because she'd never heard anything like it come out of her friend's mouth.

"Your mother would have been in jail if the authorities had known what was going on in your house," Phyllis said.

"For child neglect and even worse, child endangering. Just for starters."

Sophie didn't know about that. But even the idea that her mother could have been imprisoned for Sophie's upbringing provided an odd kind of comfort. Like the mess she'd made of her life really hadn't been all her fault.

Not that she was—ever—going to be one of those people who were lifetime victims, always blaming everything that happened to them on someone else.

She might have had a rough childhood. Lots of others had had it rougher. And she was an adult now. If her life disappointed her, the fault was solely hers.

Which was why she had to take control of it. Immediately. This was her shot to get it right.

She just had to figure out what that was.

"I…" Phyllis's faltering start drew Sophie's attention. "I was told what I know about the…woman in town in confidence," Phyllis finally managed to say. "I'm struggling with what's right here. But I do think the woman in question wasn't doubting you, Sophie. She was doubting herself.

"The conversation had nothing to do with you, any reputation you think you might have, any residuals of your past. She was talking about her own fears that she didn't have what it took to keep her husband interested. She didn't feel feminine. And she used the fact that she doesn't trust him around you as proof that she'd lost control of her own emotions in the situation. She was the one who was harboring inappropriate feelings—a completely unfounded jealousy—and that's why she spoke up. She was worried about herself."

Maybe. Sophie heard what Phyllis was saying. She accepted the logic. She wondered why the other woman hadn't named Ellen, or Randi, or Becca, or Caroline, or Phyllis or, heck, Tory, who was drop-dead gorgeous, instead of naming Sophie Curtis as the woman she feared around her husband.

Sophie knew the answer to that question.

She was single. And she had a reputation.

She was the type women thought of when they worried about their husbands straying.

Tory, on the other hand, was the type who had babies.

CHAPTER SIXTEEN

DUANE CALLED SOPHIE after court Thursday morning to arrange to see her in Shelter Valley that evening. On the way back to his office, he called Will to set up a golf date for the morning. Before he took any more action, he wanted Will's opinion on Burke's message. Duane's third call was to Allen Newsome to make peace.

"I've been acting a bit out of character," he said. "I realized, once I'd calmed down, that it was my own damn fault you'd jumped to the conclusion you had. I'm the one who kept Sophie hidden without even a mention that I was seeing someone."

"No harm done," Allen said, his voice as congenial as always. "I recognize the signs, man, and you have my sympathy."

"What signs?"

"You're in love. And at our age, that kind of upheaval's got to be tough."

Duane didn't want to think about that. But the comment reminded him of another reason for this call.

"So what about you?" he asked. "Things okay at home?"

"Fine. Why?"

"You asked about Sophie."

"You know how it is," Allen said. "You get to be our age,

thinking that life is passing you by. When I heard about your lunch date, I was so envious, I knew you'd hit the right answer again. I figured a little discreet something on the side was what I needed."

"But you know it's not, right?"

Allen's sigh wasn't encouraging. "I know logically that a fling with someone younger won't fix the problem—not in the long run. I'm still getting one day older every single day I wake up. The years will pass and at some point my body's going to ache too much to want a sweet young thing. But if I can prolong the time between now and the inevitable—"

"At what cost, man?" Duane asked. "You get that invincible feeling long enough to have an orgasm, or for whatever moments in your week you manage to sneak away. But you risk losing everything you've worked your entire life to achieve. You risk losing the woman who'll be by your side, holding you when your body aches, loving you in spite of the wrinkles and nose hairs."

Duane believed what he was saying. Completely. He'd simply never thought about such things before now. No career could ever be that kind of companion in later years.

"You're right, of course," Allen said. "And who knows if I'd ever do anything even if I had the chance. But the possibility has sure given me a lift this week."

"Make damn sure that's all you do—think about it," Duane said. He didn't have enough clout with Allen to make a difference in the man's life one way or the other.

Allen was a smart man.

But then, so was Duane, usually, and he hadn't done so well in the romance department, either.

SOPHIE HADN'T MEANT TO BE sitting on James's porch Thursday afternoon, drinking lemonade and listening to the fifty-four-year-old man's advice about life. One minute she'd been in her backyard, pressing the button on her 2.4 gallon air compressor to shoot sixteen ounces of sawdust into the air through a small metal pipe she'd purchased that morning at the hardware store. The next minute she hadn't been.

Sawdust had a natural component that was explosive. A component that, when mixed with, say, hair spray, could not only create one heck of an explosion, but could, potentially, start a fire, as well.

She needed the explosion, the raining of dust, for a desert war scene she was creating. But fire danger was out.

Her experiments with the precise mixture to create the effect had been progressing well when the air compressor hose blew loose, causing the coupler to fly up and hit her just behind her left ear.

Sophie's frightened yelp had caught James's attention, and thankfully, his orange-picking ladder was leaning against the side of his house and he'd been over the wall before Sophie had even figured out what'd happened.

She hadn't lost consciousness. Nor was she bleeding. Just dazed. Mostly due to shock.

But James, spouting words like *concussion* and *just to be safe,* wouldn't hear of her being inside alone. Instead, he'd walked her—the long way around the block—to his house. When she balked and said she didn't feel comfortable going inside his house with him, they compromised with a seat on his back porch.

He'd said she should drink something with sugar, because of the dizziness, and asked her to converse with him until it was apparent she really was fine.

His other option was calling the paramedics.

Who would take her to the clinic, where it soon would be known that she was pregnant. They'd ask all the usual questions, probably want to prescribe a painkiller. And when the obstetrician was called into her room, it would be all over town.

With the two choices at hand—James's patio or certain discovery—Sophie agreed to walk to his porch and sit for one glass of lemonade.

Then she was going back to work.

Work was good. Work had saved her before.

And would again.

Twenty minutes later, after absorbing car buying tips, investment recommendations, air compressor suggestions, water pressure advice and a full glass of lemonade, she was still on James's patio, absorbing the sunshine. Enjoying these much-needed moments of relaxation and conversation that held absolutely no expectations.

James didn't care about her past. Or her future. He had no investment in her life. Or the life inside her.

No reason to judge.

"So tell me why a nice-looking woman like you spends her time giving life lessons to other people's kids instead of her own," James said as he refilled her glass.

The sense of security she'd been lulled into vanished. But not in time to prevent a response from flowing out when she should have kept her own counsel and gone home.

"I'm not ready to have children," she said, with only a hint of defensiveness—and a truckload of truth.

This baby was her business. Until she was ready to tell Duane. After she had a plan.

"Hogwash." The comeback kind of surprised her. As if

the man knew her well enough to have an opinion. "I've heard the three of you over there, laughing and playing and talking frankly about life. Those kids come up with questions that would stop me in my tracks, and you take them on as though they were nothing more than a request for a glass of water."

"I'm used to them." Sophie was quick to assure him. James didn't know. Didn't have any idea.

"I saw them at Wal-Mart with a couple who I'm assuming were their parents," James said. "A redheaded woman and a tall, kind of serious-looking guy."

"Yeah, that's Matt and Phyllis Sheffield. They're good friends of mine. I helped out a lot after the twins were born, and the togetherness kind of stuck."

"You spend a good bit of time with them."

"Yeah."

"You love them."

"Of course."

"Like I said, you should have kids of your own to play cornhole and tag and have burping contests with."

Blushing, Sophie laughed. "I'm sorry you overheard that little episode," she said. "I generally stick to good manners when I'm with them."

Shrugging, James crossed one tennis shoe over his knee. He was really in quite good shape for someone who seemed to hang around all day.

"I expect burping contests happen quite naturally in a close family unit," he said. "They are, after all, a part of life."

"You talk like you don't know about family units," she said. "Don't you have one?"

"Nope."

"Have you ever been married?"

"Once. A long time ago. I was just out of college and had been offered a premier position at a firm I'd been scoping out for several years. I was young and full of myself…and was unfaithful to my wife."

For some reason, Sophie was really disappointed, as though she had some personal stake in this man's life decisions. As if she'd been stupid enough to heroize him, to set him up as the one man who wasn't like all the rest: ready and willing to jump into bed regardless of the morning after.

"I told her about it as soon as it happened, told her how sorry I was, and promised to stay chained to her feet forever. I even resorted to begging, but she would have none of it. I'd desecrated something she'd held most precious between us. She moved out immediately and had me served with divorce papers within the month."

"What about the other woman?"

"Never saw or heard from her again. She'd been a receptionist at the firm. One night I was there alone, working late. She came in, got out the whiskey I kept for entertaining clients, and before I knew it, she was kissing me. Afterward, I was sick about what I'd done. I couldn't believe it had happened. She wasn't too pleased with my reaction, but I had much bigger worries on my mind. I rushed home and confessed. When my wife left, I took the week off, tried to pull myself, my life, back together. By the time I returned to the office, the other woman had quit. Moved on. Guess once she knew I wasn't going to be her meal ticket, she had no reason to stick around."

"Do you have any idea what ever happened to your wife?"

"Yep. Six months after she left, she married some bloke she met at church. They've got five kids."

How sad for James.

"And you never met anyone else?"

He shook his head. "I never really looked. Thing is, I adored my wife. Truly adored her. When I lost her, no one else did the trick. And after a while, I realized that I wasn't interested for another reason."

Sophie had no business digging into James's personal life. "Which was?" she asked anyway.

"I couldn't take a chance on breaking another woman's heart. If I was capable of being unfaithful to Alicia, who was the love of my life, I couldn't trust myself to be faithful to anyone else."

He was paying for his mistake.

Because sometimes they were just that big.

THE CONVERSATION DRIFTED on to less serious topics as James told Sophie a bit about his business success—how he'd dedicated his life to his career—without ever really telling her what that career had been.

"Enough about me. Tell me about this guy you're seeing."

"Why?" He was hitting a little too close to home now.

"Just wondering if there's a connection between him and you not having kids."

"Nope."

"Does he want kids?"

"Maybe. There are other things that would have to be worked out first."

She wasn't going to tell him anything pertinent. Anything personal. She didn't reveal that much about herself. Not even to Duane.

And proximity had already let James see too much.

But neither was she ready to go back home to face the silence that was deafening her with constant demands for decisions, for plans, for choices she didn't completely trust herself to make.

"We've been struggling a bit." The words just came out. Maybe the blow to her head had affected her more than she'd realized. But totally out of character for her, over the next half hour, Sophie told this kind, older gentleman about her mother's many husbands, the way she traded up anytime she met a man who was better off than the one she had. Sophie told about husband number three and his groping fingers.

"The bastard," James spat. "I hope he was strung up by his balls and—" He lowered his head. "I'm sorry. That was no way to talk in front of a lady."

It was the perfect segue into the next phase of her life, and the men she'd liaisoned with during the search for her own brand of happiness. She didn't give details, simply said, "As it turned out, I wasn't much different from her. Mom had men in her quest for security. I had them in my quest to be loved."

"What about your father?" James asked. "Was he in the picture at all?"

She shook her head, then wished she hadn't. "I have no memory of him," she said. "He left when I was two."

"Left?"

"He was my mom's first husband and the only one who left her."

"She told you that?"

"Yeah. He was the reason for everything that went wrong in her life. Anytime she wasn't happy, or had an affair go south, she'd blame it on the fact that my dad left her alone with a baby to raise."

"Did she ever work?"

"Not that I can remember. She always said that a mother's job was to be there when her kid got home from school."

"And was she? Home when you got there?"

"Not often. She was into the country-club scene. Volunteered a lot. Guess it made her feel good about herself."

"And you never heard from your dad? Not once?"

"Nope."

"Did he send support at least?"

"If he did, I never knew about it." Sophie remembered the times she'd begged God to send her word from her father, as though that loser could somehow save her from the life of losers she already had. "I don't think he did. Mom didn't ever talk bad about him—other than for leaving us. She seemed to really love him. I've always thought so, anyway."

She'd always believed that her father was better than any of the lechers who came after. That she was somehow better because of that.

"I wrote to him once, between husbands three and four." She told James something she'd only ever told Phyllis. "Mom gave me his address."

"And?"

"He never wrote back."

"And you never tried to get in touch with him again?"

"He knew where I was. If he wanted to see me, he would have. And why, if he didn't want to see me, would I want to see him?"

James was quiet for a few seconds, then said, "Do you think it's possible that your…affection for this Duane guy is some kind of father-replacement thing?"

"Absolutely not!" She didn't even have to think about that. "I know it's odd that I'm involved with a man who's eighteen years older than I am. But believe me, I've had enough experience to know that my feelings for him are completely woman to man."

"So what's the problem?"

Sighing, Sophie gave up trying to hold anything back. "I've done it again," she said. "Here I thought I'd changed, that after so many years of being without a man, I was cured of any residual subconscious attachment to the person I'd thought I was when I was in college. I'd been through counseling. Made a success of my life.

"Then I met Duane. In a bar. In the little casino outside of town, actually. I'd come home from a particularly long and grueling job and couldn't bear the emptiness at my place. He'd lost a case he'd invested his heart and soul in. We drank too much. And rather than having him drive back to Phoenix, I invited him home with me to sleep it off. We made love that night. That very first night."

She told James that Duane had asked her to marry him. For real. That he'd given her a key to his apartment. And how things hadn't been the same between them since she'd picked that key up off the table.

She didn't tell him about the baby growing inside her.

"I'm beginning to remind myself of my mother again," she finished. Far more than he knew, because she was soon to be a single mother.

"You aren't your mother," James said, as though life really was so simple. "I can't speak to your dependency issues in the past, but one thing's pretty clear now. You aren't a dependent person. You know you can take care of yourself. You'd be able to take care of your children, too, whether it worked out with their father or not. Not that I'm purporting any kind of single-parenthood nonsense. Fathers are important. I'm simply saying, as a safety net, if something ever happened to the father of your children, you know you wouldn't become your mother."

She wasn't a dependent person.

"You said a few minutes ago that you hadn't changed, that when you met Duane in that bar, you were exactly the woman you'd been before. I don't see it." James hadn't moved from his relaxed position, wasn't filling his voice with conviction or power. His quiet, contemplative tone captured her attention.

"You would have accepted Duane's first proposal of marriage if you had been. You'd have pushed to be included in his Phoenix life. You'd have drawn him more completely into yours. Isn't that what your mother would have done?"

And insisted on joint bank accounts and a will, bequeathing all to her, too.

Sophie hadn't even thought about bank accounts. Or wills. Not in terms of her relationship with Duane.

Huh.

She didn't need a man to take care of her.

She could take care of herself.

CHAPTER SEVENTEEN

WORK CONSUMED DUANE Thursday afternoon, demanding his complete focus. He had two cases going to trial in the next week, both of which contained child custody issues and substantial amounts of money. Susan, his paralegal, had discovered discrepancies in one of the defendant's finances—inequities that would greatly reduce the financial strain on the plaintiff, Duane's client. He had his strategy, and made a list of proof that his client, Deandra Simmons, and Susan had four days to compile.

Even with everything occupying his mind, he thought about Sophie. Missed her.

More so as he spoke with Deandra, who listened to his advice, agreed to give Susan the necessary information and to meet him in his office before court, all without a single word of complaint. She was desperate. Down. Humiliated and frightened as she attempted to rebuild a shattered life.

Duane had heard it all before, in varying forms. Hundreds of times. Sometimes there were crooks, jerks, bastards involved. But most often his cases involved two people who'd expected to love and be loved by their spouse for the rest of their lives, only to have the love die. Most often his cases involved sorting through two sides of a sad story. He'd long ago learned to be compassionate without taking personal ownership of others' emotions.

But this time, listening to his client's shaking voice, all Duane could think about was Sophie sounding so lost, so frightened and shocked and…beaten.

He'd rather grow old alone than risk doing that to her.

The only call he took was at three that afternoon when Sophie's name flashed up.

"Hey, babe, I miss you," he said, his heart as full of warmth for her as his head was full of confusion and doubts about them.

"I miss you, too."

She sounded different. Not bad, necessarily. But odd.

"What's up?"

"You still coming here tonight?" she asked.

He tensed. "I was planning to. Why?"

"I… It's just—"

"What?"

"I'm not feeling so well."

Was she blowing him off?

Duane rejected the possibility the second it occurred to him. That wasn't Sophie's way. She might very well be preparing to end their liaison, but she'd do it right. In person.

And he wouldn't blame her. He'd go quietly.

He hoped.

"What's wrong?" he asked.

"I had a bit of an accident," she said, instilling instant frustration that he was an hour away.

"But I'm fine," she assured him, after explaining what had happened. "Phyllis was by a little bit ago and called the clinic. I have no signs or symptoms to worry about, and have stayed awake since the accident. I just have a bit of a headache and am sick to my stomach. The thought of making dinner makes me nauseous and—"

"Then don't." He'd asked for real life with her and this was real. "Then don't."

"But you'd need to eat and—"

"Soph, we've talked about trying to be more than just lovers, right?"

"Yeah." If she sounded too hesitant for his liking, he had no one to blame but himself.

"Then relax and let me be your partner tonight, okay? I'll take care of dinner. Maybe you'll be able to handle a little soup or something. And I'll take care of you, too."

"Okay." He wished she sounded a little more confident about the idea.

"I'll pack up here and be on my way," he said, already gathering files he could work on that night. "You rest until I get there."

"Okay."

She sounded half-asleep already. And Duane couldn't get to her fast enough.

IT WASN'T THE TWO OF THEM anymore. Wasn't ever going to be just the two of them. Their little world had been permanently invaded.

Sophie tried to push the thoughts away. But as she sat at her table that evening, watching Duane put the finishing touches on his homemade soup, her mind seemed to be only on one track.

She didn't have a plan. But she was going to tell Duane about the baby. He deserved to know.

Taking a deep breath, she swallowed the words along with the scent of dinner. The soup smelled good, and she was hungry.

And eating for two.

She'd tell him. Right after dinner.

The resident in her belly either liked potato soup as much as she did or slept through the meal. Sophie wasn't in a frame of mind to question the quiet from her midsection as she ate without any trace of nausea.

Too bad she couldn't quiet her thoughts so easily.

Candidate for state representative impregnates girl young enough to be his daughter.

Duane Koch finds out he was playing for keeps.

Love tryst lands prominent Phoenix lawyer in hot water.

Phoenix politician accused of being father of prostitute's baby.

"You're awfully quiet." He'd emptied his bowl and gone back for seconds.

"Yeah."

"Does your head hurt?"

"A little."

"Can I get you some aspirin?"

Could pregnant women take aspirin? "No, thanks. This is delicious, by the way."

"Thanks."

She spooned up another mouthful. Took a bite of one of the bread sticks he'd heated.

She loved this man. Not just as a lover. Or a part-time companion.

Out of the blue, the distinction became clear. There were no flashing lights or gonging cymbals, simply a quiet dawning of truth.

He ate. She ate. Spoons scraped against earthenware bowls, serenading them.

Watching Duane eat food he'd prepared was nothing new. They'd sat this way countless times. Something she'd taken for granted.

Tonight, knowing she might be sitting at her table with him for the last time—at least as his lover—she understood how much these moments meant to her.

Not just a lover. Not just a part of her life. But *the* man in her life.

The clarity made everything else so much more murky.

Her bowl was empty. His was almost so.

She and Duane had so much against them, and if they couldn't find a way to be together on their own, adding a baby to the mix certainly wasn't going to help. As a matter of fact, it would hurt almost every aspect of the challenges they faced.

"Is this what we've come to?" Resting his spoon in the empty bowl, Duane sat back, clasping his hands behind his head. "Having so little to say to each other that we have to eat in silence?"

They were hurting each other. And it was only going to get worse. Sometimes love wasn't enough.

"Duane…" She wanted to offer comfort. To make everything okay. "My bulimia didn't come back. At least, not as severely as I'd thought. Not enough to make me throw up."

"It didn't? That's great, Soph…." His voice faded. "How do you know? You had the flu?" he asked slowly, frowning.

"No. I'm pregnant."

Bracing herself, literally, by clutching the chair beside her thighs, Sophie waited.

And waited some more.

Duane was looking at her, but she wasn't sure he saw

her. And she had no idea, from the blank expression on his face, what he was thinking.

Was he angry? Was he worried that she'd been unfaithful to him, because they'd always been so careful and you couldn't get pregnant through a condom?

Did he feel any softer feelings at all? Any tenderness at the idea of a little life growing inside her?

"I…uh, I have no idea what to say." He didn't sound mad. His hands dropped to his lap. "Or what to do, either."

She'd tackle what she could. "There's really nothing for you to do," she assured him. "You just needed to know."

Chin jutted out, he nodded, as though in agreement with the statement. "How long have *you* known?"

"Since Tuesday afternoon."

"Who else knows?"

"No one."

"This changes everything."

Yeah, that's what she'd been afraid of.

"WE'RE GOING TO HAVE TO get married." Duane's mind was mostly empty as he stared at Sophie. Which made the one or two thoughts he did have very clear.

She was shaking her head. He didn't like that. And didn't understand it, either.

"Soon," he continued. "As soon as possible."

"Duane, we aren't getting married."

"We have to."

"No, we don't."

"Of course we do."

She shook her head again. Maybe the bump she'd taken had done more damage than he'd thought.

He leaned forward, and noticed his hands folded neatly

on the table in front of him. He hadn't realized he'd put them there. "Sophie," he said slowly, as if explaining the law to a client who wasn't understanding that she couldn't automatically sue her husband for everything he had because he didn't love her anymore. "We're having a baby. We're going to be parents."

Chills ran through him. Oh God. He was going to be a father. A dad. As in a man with a little baby in his arms. A toddler holding his finger. A son whom he'd have to teach about safe sex. Or a daughter he'd have to protect from all of the avaricious, sex-crazed men in the world.

How could he do that? He lived alone in a luxury condo that a child would destroy in a day.

"I'm telling you, Soph, we have to get married."

"Look—" she covered his hands with hers "—I'm not saying that we won't." Her voice was soft. Nurturing. Like a warm blanket covering the coldness inside him. "Eventually. But not until we work out the other issues we've been having. You know as well as I do that getting married for the sake of a child is stupid. We'd be asking for disaster."

Okay. He'd buy that. "So let's work them out."

"I'd like that."

He waited. She didn't say anything else.

"Now."

"What do you mean, *now?*"

"I mean now, tonight. Let's get them worked out."

Her chuckle startled him. And lowered his blood pressure a little bit. "Duane, if it were that easy, don't you think we'd have done something already?"

She was right. The rest of the world descended on him, reminding him that he was a candidate for public office. And she was twenty-eight years old. And...

"Can we move to the couch?" He didn't have any answers. But he needed to be close to her.

Taking the hand he offered, Sophie let him lead her to the couch, then pull her against him. She let him sit there, silent, mulling over life, over his lack of answers.

"Hard to believe," he said eventually—his understatement of the year. "We were so careful."

"Yeah." She leaned her head back, nestling it between his shoulder and the couch. "I'm never regular, you know that, and we *are* careful, so it wasn't an issue. But after I talked to Tory I started to worry, and you know once thoughts get started you run with them. I was driving myself crazy and finally got the test just so I'd quit worrying. Except that it shocked me instead."

"And you got scared."

"Maybe."

"And thought about all the ramifications for my career, and the press and—"

"Gold Digger Uses Oldest Trick in the Book to Trap Wealthy Attorney," she interrupted dryly.

And silence fell again.

"I wonder if he'll have blond hair or dark." After more than fifteen minutes of nothing it was the best he could come up with.

"Or if he'll be a she."

"Dark's dominant."

It took him a while to realize she never replied. Until she shifted and he remembered that she'd been having problems with nausea. Morning sickness. The term took on an all-new meaning. "How are you feeling?"

"Fine."

"You sure?"

"Mmm-hmm."

And he wondered if they could sit like this, wrapped together on her couch, in calm silence, for the rest of their lives. And leave the world outside.

"I HAVE A SUGGESTION to make." Duane's voice startled Sophie. She had no idea what time it was, how long they'd been sitting there on her couch. Her legs were stiff, but she didn't bother straightening them.

"What's that?"

"That we go ahead full force with our original plan. You come to Phoenix, spend time with me. And we spend time in Shelter Valley, only we go out together, go to church, see your friends together."

Tension tightened her chest, making it hard to breathe.

"We tackle the issues head-on, just like we said we would. And, at least at first, we keep the baby to ourselves. Or within our private circle here in Shelter Valley."

She saw where he was going with this. The only place they could go, really, if they were going anywhere together at all. They had to try. Or let their relationship die. Wasn't that the crossroads they'd been at for weeks?

Deciding whether to try or let it die?

"And what happens if it doesn't work?"

"We find a way to part."

"But by then your public will know about me, and when I turn up pregnant, they'll know the baby is yours, and have a field day with all three of us."

"They're going to know that eventually, Sophie. There's no way I'm going to be a silent father in my child's life."

He sounded awfully certain about that.

"Like it or not, we made a baby." Duane's tone gave no

indication of what he was feeling. "We owe it to this child to give life together a fair shot."

The cacophony that had been flying around inside of Sophie for two days settled.

"We were already here, Sophie," Duane continued, and she felt a twinge of sympathy for anyone who was up against him in court. "We already knew, on some level, that what we've had these past two years is important to both of us. Important enough that neither one of us broke it off. Neither one of us has been able to walk away. Maybe that something that kept us coming back to each other is the something that will see us through whatever is to come."

"Maybe."

"So, we have a deal?"

Her head hurt. Suddenly, lying here with him, knowing that she wasn't completely alone with her overwhelming life change, she was so tired she could hardly keep her eyes open. "I guess."

Not sure that she hadn't just opened up both her and Duane to more heartache, to a prolonging of the inevitable, to more pain than either of them knew, Sophie let him lead her to bed. And when he pulled her against him, gave her a kiss on the head and told her to get some rest, she went to sleep.

HE WAS GOING TO BE a father.

Duane knew now why Sophie had been so distant the past couple of days. He picked an iron. Drove. Made his second birdie of the morning.

"How's Sophie?" Will asked after they'd teed off on the third hole. "Any repercussions?"

It took Duane a second to catch up. And to slow down.

Will knew nothing about the baby. He was referring to her mishap with the air compressor the day before.

"I'm guessing Phyllis called Becca," Duane said.

"No, Martha did. Phyllis called Martha to let her know that Sophie wouldn't be stopping by with the stage plan she was working up for this year's Shelter Valley Days."

Shaking his head at the speed with which information traveled in this town—making him feel doubly uncomfortable that he'd impregnated someone outside of wedlock—Duane said, "She didn't even have a headache this morning. She's got a respectable knot on the side of her head, though." He'd helped her fix her hair to cover it.

Then, after he'd extracted her promise that she'd meant what she said the night before about giving life in Phoenix a try, he'd quickly kissed her goodbye and left.

Hopefully before she got an inkling of the doubts that had been keeping him up all night.

He wanted Sophie in his life. Forever. He just wasn't sure he was ready to have her in Phoenix. He wasn't sure he was ready to have her pay that price.

Or to pay the price himself.

On the third green, with Will one stroke behind Duane, the college president asked, "I'm assuming there's a reason that you keep sighing and pursing your lips?"

Will lined up his shot. Duane said nothing.

"You got a hard case this morning?" Will asked, missing the hole on his first putt.

There were some things a man didn't talk to other men about. Like how inept he felt at the thought of keeping a wife happy, let alone the thought of fatherhood.

What the hell did Duane know about kids? He could hardly remember being one.

Will made his second putt. Picked up his ball. Backed off the green. "Troubles between you and Sophie?" His quietly uttered statement reached Duane as he lined up his own putt.

He sank the ball. Put the pin back in the hole. Will wasn't going to relent. And that's when Duane thought of Michael Burke. When one problem gets too tough, switch to another.

"What do you really think about my running for state representative?" he asked as they approached the next tee.

"You know what I think."

They set down their bags, side by side.

"That I'm the best man for the job. Yeah, I know. But is that because you think I'm good for the job, or because there aren't other good choices?"

Will peered over at him. "What is it you really want to know?"

Duane wasn't an in-touch guy. Or one who admitted having emotions to another man.

But he was driving himself insane. He remembered when Will had come to him all those years ago, struggling with emotions he didn't have a damned idea what to do with.

Duane hadn't known, either.

But they'd had a helluva good game of cards. And way too many beers.

He could do with one now. Instead, he looked his friend straight in the eye. "Do you think I'm ethical?" So his chin was jutting. This wasn't easy.

"Hell, yes! What brought that on?"

"I wonder about myself lately," Duane admitted, pulling out a five iron for the par three facing them. "What kind of man fights so vocally for what he believes in, and hides away an important part of his life for two solid years?"

Will grabbed a seven iron. "We're talking about Sophie."

"Yes."

"You're facing a delicate balancing act." Will put his ball on the tee, then leaned on his club. "Your career goals are almost twenty years in the making. A lot of people have been involved in grooming you for this position. They're depending on you. And a lot more stand to benefit from your work once you get elected."

Nothing Duane hadn't already told himself.

"But you've also managed to acquire a personal life. Unfortunately, the two lives aren't coinciding. There's not a damn thing unethical about that. The way I see it, you're trying to do the best you can for both of your worlds."

Will's drive was impressive, landing just short of the green.

"Am I?" Duane asked. He put his ball down, and slammed it so far down the fairway it sailed over the hole. "Or am I being weak? Lazy? Have I cashed in on the fact that Sophie's so accommodating and made choices that are best for me, without considering what was best for her?"

"I don't know," Will said. "Have you?"

Duane wished he could be sure. Wished he could be perfect and get it over with.

"What's going to happen when I put her out on public display?" he asked. "Aside from what the press might do to us, what my relationship with her might do to her reputation—and mine."

And now there was a baby to add to that mix. He and Sophie couldn't catch a break.

"What do you mean? What else is there aside from that?"

"I'll have to share her with the world."

Will swung. Made a birdie.

Duane congratulated him. Found his ball. "I'm a jealous

old fool," he said, taking two shots to get his ball in the hole, maintaining a one-point lead.

"Because I outputt you?"

"Because I want Sophie all to myself." And now her baby, too. *Their* baby. "When all I have to do is be there for her, alone, I know I'm good. Enter other things, and I'm not so sure." Enter other men. Finding her attractive. Enter snide remarks about his age. And hers. Enter a lost chance at a career he'd been working toward forever. Enter anything else she might need that he might not be able to give her. He was at an all-time low. Humiliated in his inability to set things straight. Whining like a sap. And still, when Will said nothing, Duane continued. "She's got this guy living behind her for the winter—"

"James Benson. Yeah, I know," Will said. "He was here yesterday morning. I ran into him coming off the putting green."

"And?"

"Seems nice enough. Well-spoken. Says he's on sabbatical."

"From what?"

"He didn't say and I didn't ask."

"I think he has a thing for Sophie."

"I wouldn't know about that."

"I told her she had to quit seeing him."

"I'm guessing that went over well."

Uh-huh.

"Let me ask you this," Will said, drawing out a wood for the next par four. "Do you really believe that Sophie would go to bed with another man? Her temporary neighbor, or anyone else?"

"No." Not while she was committed to Duane. But the

more involved they became, the more they shared aspects of their lives, the more chance he had to screw up.

And when he failed, would she stay committed?

Hell, he'd already let her down. He'd hidden her away like something that shamed him, while she'd given him a key to her home—and to her heart. And she hadn't been unfaithful to him.

Of course, in his business, he saw how often those keys broke. Or were changed.

All these years, he'd prided himself on having such compassion for his clients, when all the while he hadn't had a clue. Unlike him, his clients were people who'd risked everything. Since his brief marriage when he was still a kid, Duane had gone for the sure thing every time. The sure win.

"Forgive me if I'm overstepping my bounds here, but I think the answers you're struggling to find all rest with you, my friend," Will said, lining up his shot. "Faith and trust come from an inner ability to believe in something unseen, to expect it to be there without ever having proof that it is. Maybe that's too much of a stretch for a man who spends his days accepting nothing without proof."

Maybe Duane really didn't have what it took to give Sophie what she needed. What she deserved.

He played out the front nine and won by one stroke. Then drove to Phoenix and the life that had sustained him for two decades. It wasn't until he'd arrived that he remembered he'd been intending to tell Will about his dinner with Michael Burke. A sure sign that he wasn't himself. A warning that he'd best get his personal life under control.

One thing was for certain. He needed this campaign. He might never make a good life partner, a good husband, a good father, but he was completely certain he'd make a good lawmaker.

CHAPTER EIGHTEEN

LOOKING AT THE FIGURES in front of her, Sophie punched numbers into the calculator again. Adding columns, so much fabric at so much a yard, shouldn't be this difficult. But then she had to account for the overage she'd need for the half scrim in the third scene. And the combination she was using for the fifth and—

Music blared from the other side of the room. It took her a second to recognize the sound as her cell phone's ring tone. Then another couple of beats to reach the thing and see Duane's name on the screen.

"Hey."

"How are you?"

"Good." The same answer she'd given him an hour ago when he'd called on his way to the office.

"No morning sickness?"

"Not so far." Last call, he'd wanted to know what she'd had for breakfast.

"Good. Did you phone a doctor?"

He'd asked if she'd consider choosing a Phoenix obstetrician rather than the one in Tucson.

"Yeah. I have an appointment the first Tuesday after my Colorado trip."

"Nothing sooner?"

"Apparently we're the only ones who feel a huge urgency. Since I've barely missed a period, and have no need for abortion counseling, I can wait a few weeks."

She was kind of glad for the reprieve. For the chance to settle into the idea of being a mother before the practical process of becoming one began. And for the chance for her and Duane to settle, too, one way or the other. If she was going to be doing this alone, she'd just as soon start that way with her first visit. Less messy. Less explaining to do.

"Listen, I had a message from my campaign manager this morning. There might be a meeting sometime tomorrow."

"Early?"

"I'm not sure. So…why don't you come to Phoenix tonight?"

"Or we could wait until you confirm the meeting."

"Soph, if we're going to try this, we have to start."

He was right, of course. She was simply a lot more comfortable having him come to Shelter Valley. Or she could always say she'd changed her mind. That she didn't want to try.

"Okay. What time do you want me?"

"I want you all the time." His voice had lowered, and suddenly he was her Duane again. For that second, everything felt completely right.

THE CONDO SMELLED delicious. Track lighting over the wall-mounted, flat-screen television softly illuminated the immense living space. The drawn floor-to-ceiling, electric-track drapes were parted enough to reveal the glittering lights around the lake, at Arizona State University and Phoenix beyond. An MP3 unit played soft rock tunes in the background. Clean, six-hundred-thread-count sheets covered the king-size bed beneath a handwoven comforter and an array of down pillows. The plush towels in the adjoining bath matched, hanging neatly beside the sunken hot tub. His shoes were lined up for once, side by side, with all toes touching the rear molding of the closet. And his loose change was put away in the milk jug in the spare room closet.

Duane had called Flora in for an extra cleaning, and though he checked, he didn't find a spot of dust anywhere. Which was saying something for a condo in the middle of the desert. Even a citified desert.

When Sophie called, as he'd asked her to do once she turned off the freeway into Tempe, he rode the elevator down and waited outside for her to pull in.

He was going to tell her tonight about Michael Burke's reaction to Duane's association with her. If they had any chance at all of making this relationship work, they were going to have to be completely honest and up-front with each other. Secrets left room for doubt. And doubt, especially when the press would be printing half-truths and innuendos, was something they could not afford.

He saw her car and stood upright, not quite as unaffected as he tried to appear. They might have a tough night ahead of them, a tough year, but she was entering her—possibly—new home for the first time.

At least a ceremonial introduction to the doorman was in order.

"HOW ABOUT IF WE MOVE over to the couch?"

Sophie was still at the table, feeling awkward while Duane finished the dishes he'd insisted on doing himself—a treat for her first night in Phoenix, he'd said.

She'd thought maybe he preferred to be the one handling his possessions, putting dishes away. He knew where they belonged, how he liked his things kept.

The fingers of his left hand were twitching. As though he was nervous about something. She was nervous, too. Uncharacteristically so.

Until Duane sat next to her. His closeness, the familiar woodsy scent of his aftershave, added some of the warmth that had been missing all evening. No matter where they were, this was still Duane. Her lover. The man she loved. Regardless of how she felt, she was not a woman on a deserted island.

"I have something to tell you then something to ask you," he said. He sat close but didn't quite touch her. His glance moved to the view of the city in front of them, then back to her.

Sophie tried to focus on that view, to pick out a familiar landmark. Chase Field. Or the airport. The Arizona Center. To find anything real about the fancy condo in which she sat. It was lovely.

And sterile.

Where were the pictures? The memorabilia? A paper or two lying around? Anything that spoke of the man she knew rather than the decorator he'd so obviously hired.

This condo did reflect Duane—or at least his life in Phoenix. His life without her.

He'd told her so often enough. Told her that, other than his career, he'd lived an empty existence.

He needed her. Needed the life she brought to him.

Sophie slid a hand onto his thigh. "What did you have to tell me?" she asked softly.

When he looked at her, his dark brown eyes had an emotional sheen she hadn't seen in a while.

"We're going to be completely open and honest, right?"

Watching her, he nodded. Duane's palm covered the back of her hand, pressing her flesh more firmly into his thigh. "That dinner I had with Michael Burke the other night…"

"Yeah?" With all that had happened, she'd pretty much forgotten about his dinner.

"It wasn't a campaign planning session as I'd assumed."

"Oh?" Was that foreboding in his voice? "What was it?"

"My good friend and associate giving me a warning." He gave her what she suspected was the digest version of the conversation.

Had his hand not been holding hers in place, Sophie would have pulled away. It was starting already, after only one stolen lunch together. The situation was bad.

Worse than she'd feared.

And that was before the baby. Before her past came out. As Duane spoke, one thing was becoming more and more clear to Sophie.

She had to be prepared to let him go.

AS CLOSELY AS HE COULD remember, Duane relayed the dinner conversation he'd had two nights before. Laid it out for her as it had happened, with no interjections of his own thoughts, because he wanted Sophie to be fully aware, fully versed on everything they faced, every step they might take over the next several months. He ended with his statement that he would just have to take his chances.

"You can't do that." Her initial response didn't surprise him. "We've waited two years, Duane. What's one more?"

As he received the response he'd expected, a suspicion

occurred to him that he didn't like much—that didn't make him too fond of himself. Was it possible he'd related the exchange exactly as it happened because he'd known she'd let him off the hook? He was a master manipulator in the courtroom.

And in life, as well?

"This is good, really," Sophie said. "It's taken everything out of our hands before we made it too messy. Life has a way of giving us what we need sometimes, when we're too blind or befuddled to take care of matters for ourselves. Maybe this year is what we need. It will give us time for me to have the baby and—"

"No!" He'd never spoken so sharply to Sophie before. "I'm sorry," he said as soon as he took his next breath. "But no, Soph."

So much for using his manipulative powers. She'd handed him a way out and he'd tossed it back.

She was teasing her lower lip with her teeth. Something he'd never seen her do before.

"I think you're partially right," he amended. He was winging it here. But the thoughts, the words kept coming. "Life does hand us gifts in disguise sometimes, little helpmates along the way. And this was definitely one of them."

Her gorgeous green eyes were wide as she gazed at him. "How so?"

"Because it's forced me to make a decision in real time. I've been vacillating and doubting and wondering—not about how I feel about you—but about how we fit the rest of my life. And yours.

"And when it came right down to it, when you give me an out, I find that I don't want it. At all."

"So you decided this just now? This minute? You were thinking about backing off from us during the campaign?"

"No, Soph, I wasn't," Duane said. "But neither am I sure we're going to make it.

"What I do know is that we've done nothing wrong," he said. "We met. We enjoyed each other's company. We became close."

"We're lovers."

"And? In today's world adult couples have sex. There's no scandal here. As long as we get to the press before they get to us, make sure they have the story straight instead of putting an ugly spin on it, we could defuse things."

He was making light of the challenges facing them. Duane recognized that. But it was time to stop wallowing and move. He had something to defend here: his right to be with Sophie. Or hers to be with him if that was her choice.

He'd never actually looked at the situation from that angle.

"I'm always going to be a presence in your life, Soph, because of the baby. But I also don't want to lose *us*."

"It's okay, Duane." She pulled her hand from beneath his. "If the feelings we share are real, you won't lose us by taking a year off. This is your entire life's goal we're talking about here. Your reputation. Your livelihood."

Her words didn't bring the relief he might have expected.

"Look around you," he said, words still coming to him out of thin air—things he'd never have come up with had he planned his attack. "Do you see how I've been living for the past twenty years? See what my reputation and my livelihood do for me?"

Maybe not the best argument with the lights of Phoenix spread romantically before them.

So he did what he did best in tight situations. He kept

talking. "I used to be so proud of this place," Duane said, the debate of his life raging inside him. "I felt such a thrill when I'd come home after a long day in court and pour myself a drink and sit here and look out at the city I love. I'd tell myself I was a vital part of her. And on an occasional weekend, when I took time away from files, I'd sit over there—" he pointed to the home theater system at the other end of the room "—and watch a basketball game and think *this is the life.*"

He turned, taking both of her hands in his. "But that faded about as quickly as I got used to turning the corner to pull into the parking lot downstairs. Because as nice as all of this is, it means nothing, it's boring and empty when I'm all alone here."

"But that doesn't mean you have to move me in. Especially not right now."

"I know," he said. "I've dated women over the years. I've had parties and invited guys over for poker nights and beer and football. I'd enjoy myself, then they'd go home."

"Being lonely isn't a reason to throw all of this away."

"In the first place, I'm not throwing it all away. This condo isn't paid for by my political standing in the community," he said dryly. "As a matter of fact, the campaign is going to cost me. And I've never seen or heard one news story about a lawyer's love life. As long as I do my job well, continue to win cases, I'm going to have my livelihood.

"And in the second place, you missed my point. I could have found someone to stay here with me if I'd wanted to," he said. "When it was time for people to go home, I was ready for them to leave."

"Oh."

He couldn't help a small grin. It wasn't often he made

her speechless. Or maybe the grin was a result of how un-comfortable all of this was making him.

"The thing is, Soph, since I met you, I have not preferred my own company to yours."

"Duane." She pulled a hand free to put it back on his thigh, but the move seemed more defensive than forward. "Let's not make rash moves here. Burke's warning changes things. I'm guessing that, if not for the baby, you'd have been willing to slow things down. Maybe ask for your key back. Now, with me pregnant, you're changing your mind. But proximity is no reason to do that—"

"Sophie—"

"No, let me finish. I'm pretty sure we've got something very real and deep between us," she said. "That's obvious. As I said before, we wouldn't both be struggling so much to let go if the connection we share wasn't authentic. But that's no reason to jump into something you aren't ready for. You wanted me to give you an out. I'm giving it to you."

He might have believed she really wanted out. Might have been insecure enough to back down and let her return the key and leave. After all, life would be a hell of a lot easier if he could hit the campaign trail a whole man—or the version of whole he used to be. A man who was self-contained.

But there was that little word *you*. She'd said "Jump into something *you* aren't ready for."

Not we.

There was that other little issue: she was having his baby. He had to be responsible for his actions. Had to *take* action.

Sitting back, without a single nervous twitch in his body, Duane reached into his pocket, pulled out the ring he'd bought for her and failed to offer her.

"I'm not reacting to your presence," he said, "though I

have to admit your loveliness does things to this room that are far more valuable than anything I could ever buy to put here. And I wasn't planning to ask for your key back. On the contrary."

Duane dropped to one knee, his free hand on her leg, and gazed up into the eyes he'd like to believe he would see looking back at him first thing in the morning every day for the rest of his life.

"Sophie Curtis, will you please marry me? I want you to be my wife, for better or worse, in sickness and health, through good press and bad." He held out the full-carat diamond solitaire. "This is what I was planning to ask you tonight. I don't want your key back. I want you to have the key to my life."

He offered the ring to her. This wasn't a time for slipping it on her finger. If Sophie wanted it, she had to take it. This wasn't an easy road he was offering her.

She was tempted. He could tell by the longing in her eyes as she stared at his palm.

"I had a glass of lemonade with James Benson yesterday."

Those were the absolute last words he'd expected to hear. And yet, after the initial sting had dissipated enough for him to think, Duane understood their timing.

"How did that come about?" he asked, praying he wouldn't let himself down, wouldn't let her down, losing rational thought to another bout of insecurity.

"I cried out when I hit my head. He heard. Climbed over the wall with his cell phone, all set to call the paramedics."

Duane managed to keep a tight rein on his thoughts.

"I didn't want to call the squad, for obvious reasons, and James relented as long as I let him be assured that I wasn't concussed. He wanted me to stay awake and talk to him."

"Okay."

"We sat on his porch."

That was better than on hers, though Duane wasn't sure why.

"Did you go inside his house at all?"

"No."

"Did you have your cell phone with you?"

"Yes, I always wear it, you know that."

"Probably wasn't the smartest thing for a woman to do, sitting alone on a man's porch. But you knew him, could scream if you needed help, had your phone—"

"I was perfectly safe, Duane."

He was sure she had been.

"I appreciate that he was concerned for you."

"And what about that ring?" she asked.

"What about it?"

"You still want me to have it?"

"Yes," he said. "The next time you're in conversation with another man, he'll see my ring on your finger. A ring that says, 'Talk, but don't touch. She's committed elsewhere, to someone who's committed to her.'"

"Does it really say that?" Sophie's voice shook.

"It does. That and more. Please wear my ring, Soph."

"Oh, Duane." She stared at the diamond. At him.

"I want to," she said, tears filling her eyes. "If things were different… I'm just so afraid. And now, with the baby…"

Duane panicked. She wanted the ring, but she was going to turn him down. He lifted her left hand, kissed it, then slid his ring all the way on.

He waited, but though she fingered the jewel, she didn't take it off.

And without another word he led her to his bedroom,

prepared especially for her, and settled her in his bed, where he spent a good part of the night trying to show her with his body all the things his words had left out.

SOPHIE HAD NO IDEA what time it was. From her vantage point, lying against Duane's chest, she couldn't see a clock. Snuggled in, she didn't want to move. Didn't want to disturb him, or her sense of well-being.

The past few days had been hard. Some of the hardest of her life. And if all could be made well simply by lying close to the man she loved, then it couldn't be wrong to be with him, could it?

Surely, no matter what was to come, they'd be all right. Their child would be all right.

With a sigh that took all of the remaining tension from her body, she closed her eyes. And willed the peace she felt now to follow her through sleep and into the next weeks and months.

SOPHIE WAS SLEEPING soundly when Duane awoke in the morning. For the longest time, he stayed listening to her breathe, watching her sleep.

She was going to wake soon. And need to eat, so she didn't get sick.

He'd never had breakfast in bed before, not even at a hotel. Had never seen the sense in it.

But with Sophie in his bed, the idea took root. Had merit. If they were married, they could have breakfast in that bed anytime they wanted. Scenarios presented themselves. Not many of them had to do with the actual eating of food, at least not in any way he'd ever eaten eggs and bacon before.

Spurred by ideas that continued to pour forth, Duane had bacon on the built-in grill next to his stove, eggs in a pan and four pieces of bread in the toaster oven in less time than it normally took him to get out the milk and cereal and make his way to the table. The engorged state of his naked body beneath his hastily donned robe attested to the direction of his thoughts.

Not having anything akin to a bed tray, he pulled out a cookie sheet, covered it with cloth napkins—part of a gift from the firm when he'd moved in—and set it with silverware, two small glasses of orange juice, strawberry jam, salt and pepper and one plate.

He'd just flipped the eggs when his cell phone rang. He wasn't picking up. It was eight o'clock Saturday morning. And he was in the middle of preparing a celebration.

If it was Burke, or Sam, they'd leave a message.

But when Duane grabbed the offending instrument to shut off its cacophonous interruption before it woke Sophie, he recognized the number blinking up at him.

The Maricopa County Jail.

CHAPTER NINETEEN

AWAKE BEFORE THE PHONE rang, Sophie considered getting out of bed. She stretched across the soft mattress on Duane's side, luxuriating in the contrast created by the cool sheets beneath her and the cozy down covers snuggled over her. And tried not to drool at the tantalizing smells coming from the other room. She was ravenous. For the moment, anyway.

She heard his voice, but couldn't make out what he was saying. He didn't talk long.

Had he gotten rid of whoever had interrupted their morning?

Maybe he was coming in to wake her, so she could join him for the breakfast he'd prepared. Kind of sweet, but she loved their mornings in the kitchen together.

"You're awake." Duane sounded almost disappointed as he came through the door with a loaded cookie sheet in his hands.

"I smelled something wonderful." Sophie stacked the pillows behind her, creating a down backrest for him, as well, as he set the tray on the bed and opened the jam before sitting on the edge of the mattress.

"I'm not going to be able to join you," he said.

Sophie was disappointed, too. Incredibly. "Why not?"

"I have a client in jail. His estranged wife accused him

of hitting her, and called the police. He won't say anything to anyone until I'm there."

He spread jam on a piece of toast, then handed it to her. He doctored another one and bit into it.

"Did he do it?" She started with some bacon on the toast—in case that was all she was going to get. Her appetite was leaving already.

"No. She's pulled this type of thing before. She's vowed to see him in jail. This is the fourth call to the authorities, but the first time he's actually been arrested. The woman is nuts."

Duane cut into the eggs, fed Sophie a bite, then took one for himself.

"Are you sure about that? Maybe he's lying."

"Not Tommy. You'd have to meet him to understand. He's the gentlest guy I've ever met, which is what makes this so ludicrous. He's a greeting-card artist, and lives for his kids. He has temporary custody, by the way, until the divorce is final and he's granted permanent custody."

Taking a woman's babies away from her? Sophie hated the sound of that. "How can you take children away from their mother?"

"She left them strapped in their car seats last September for two hours while she got her hair done."

September in Phoenix was hot. In the nineties.

"And another time, after they'd been with their dad, she threw away all of their toys to punish them for being with him."

"How old are they?"

"Two and three."

A little young to be held accountable for much of anything. "Boys or girls?"

"Boys," Duane said, feeding her another bite. "She

reported Tommy for mail fraud because some junk mail addressed to him was delivered to their old address."

"Oh."

"And the last time he showed up to collect the kids, she called the cops to arrest him for trespassing. That's when we won temporary custody."

The eggs were gone. As were the bacon and toast. And soon, Duane would be, too.

He stood. "Shower with me?"

Nodding, Sophie slid from the bed. Anything to prolong this last bit of time she and Duane would have alone together. To avoid thoughts that were better left unacknowledged.

"What time will you be back?" she asked twenty minutes later, as she straightened his tie and, dressed only in his robe, with her hair wet around her ears, stood on tiptoe to kiss him goodbye.

"I'm not sure. Hopefully within the hour. Maybe longer. Make yourself at home. And when I get back—" he clasped her shoulders, kissed her long and hard, using his tongue as much as his lips "—we'll decide how we're going to make our debut and tackle this town."

"Duane?" She had to say something. Had to commit, before she lost herself in confusion and indecision.

"Yeah?"

"You still think we should do this?" Once they were out, there would be no reversing things.

A shadow of insecurity passed over his features. "I don't think we have any other choice."

Which wasn't the same thing at all.

WHEN SOPHIE HEARD the knock on the door almost three hours after Duane had left, she rushed to open it, thinking he'd left his key behind. Or in his briefcase, where he generally kept everything but the single car key he carried, to avoid bulk in his pocket. At least, when he came to Shelter Valley that was what he did. But then, in Shelter Valley he didn't need his condo key.

With security requiring a code to enter the building, and a doorman as second-tier protection, she wasn't worried about physical safety.

Until she'd pulled open the door and didn't recognize the gray-haired man, dressed in pants and a casual shirt, standing on the threshold of Duane's apartment. Her eager smile faded to one of generic welcome.

"Can I help you?"

They didn't allow solicitors in the building. Maybe the distinguished-looking man was a neighbor.

"So what Burke said was true." He said the words almost as though he was talking to himself.

Recognizing the name of Duane's party chairperson, Sophie started to panic. Wished she wore something a bit more presentable than jeans and a blouse. She and Duane didn't have a plan yet. And she didn't want to blow this for him.

She shouldn't have answered the door. He was going to kill her for doing so. Well, Duane wouldn't, he was too nice for that. But how could she have been so stupid?

"Is Duane in?" the man asked.

She wanted to say her fiancé was in the shower. But that didn't sound good. Not with her right here, as though she was often around when Duane showered. Plus it wouldn't be hard to disprove the lie. There was no water running in the condo.

Afraid the truth was somehow stamped across her face,

anyway, Sophie said, "He had to go…meet with a client. But he should be back any second. Can I have him call you?"

"I've come all the way over from Scottsdale to see him," the man said. "I'd like to wait, if I may."

She wasn't a wife yet. Didn't know her way around the apartment enough to be able to offer him drinks without first checking to see where they were. Had no idea even what was there. She didn't know how to turn on the television or stereo.

"I'm Sam Livingston, his campaign manager," the man said when she hesitated. "I can make myself at home. I helped Duane get this place. I own a couple of units here myself."

Without waiting for any further direction from her, he walked past her into the condominium. The first place Sam stopped was the kitchen, where he knew exactly the right cupboard to find the glasses, then to the refrigerator. Taking out the orange juice, he poured himself three-quarters of a glass, then proceeded to a wine cooler built into a cupboard, took out one of several bottles of champagne, popped the top and added some of the bubbly liquid to his juice.

Closing his eyes, he sipped. Smacked his lips. "Mmm." He seemed to notice her, to remember she was even there, when he opened his eyes. "There's nothing like a good mimosa to get a day off started right," he said. "Would you like one?"

Not without Duane there. And not while she was pregnant.

"No, thank you," she said, feeling about as small as the crumb she'd missed on the counter over by the toaster.

So much for her worrying about her ability to play hostess. Sam Livingston obviously was more at home here than she was. And seemed to think he had more right to be here, too.

Duane had mentioned the guy, of course, but she hadn't realized the two knew each other so well.

Because she'd never been a part of Duane's life.

"So—" Sam took a seat on the couch she'd shared with Duane last night "—tell me about yourself. Where are you from? How did you meet Duane?"

They didn't have their plan yet.

How could she, who had no experience in this political world, know what Duane would want her to say? What way would he, the master of words, have her present things to have the best effect and do the least damage?

Didn't politicians have advisors who wrote that stuff for them?

While she had no idea how to best present herself, Sophie did come from the world of theater. As part of her production degree she'd had to take some acting classes.

That training propelled her across the room to the thick leather chair positioned perpendicular to the panoramic view outside the condo. What she'd give to be out there, an invisible speck lost somewhere in the city.

There was nothing to do but answer the intimidating man's questions.

"Originally I'm from Denver," she said, her stomach in knots. What if they found her mother? Splashed her antics all over the paper? Sophie hadn't even considered that horror.

"I moved to Shelter Valley to go to Montford on full scholarship, and after graduation decided to stay."

She'd just handed him the opportunity to find out all about her past. Unwrapped and out there.

They would have found out anyway. She folded her arms across her belly, cradling the child she was beginning to accept as real.

"Montford, yes," Sam said. "Actually, I'm kind of glad

we have this opportunity to talk here, without Duane." He set down his glass to lean forward, elbows on his knees.

She crossed her legs, trying to create some space between them. "Oh, why?"

"We did some checking. Once Duane told Michael your name was Sophie it was relatively easy. We knew he spent time in Shelter Valley, that he's good friends with Will Parsons."

Sophie froze. She should have known. Duane should have known. They'd already done their digging. Too much was at stake here.

Maybe Duane did know they'd investigated her.

Maybe he hadn't told her, hadn't wanted to scare her off.

Sam shifted to the end of the couch, putting his hands within inches of her knee. He took another sip of his drink, saying nothing.

Was the silence some kind of intimidation tactic? Building her up for easy acquiescence? He was going to ask her to leave Duane. She could hear the request coming.

Little did he know that he wouldn't have to try too hard. She would never give in to the pressure if she had only herself to consider. She'd handle the press, the smear on her reputation. She knew that now.

But there wasn't only her to consider.

She had to take into account the man she loved. And their baby. Three hours alone in an unfamiliar place had given her far too much time to think.

Obviously a child needed his father, but the parents didn't have to be married.

Duane had said they'd take the press on. That they had no scandal. But as soon as it was obvious she was pregnant, even Will Parsons and the Sheffields wouldn't be at fault for thinking that the baby was the reason she and Duane were suddenly getting married. The press would, of course, put a worse slant on the liaison than would their friends, and the end result could be a nightmare. What kind of life would that be for the baby? To be dubbed little more than a trap? A pawn in a tawdry game?

And what if Duane really did start to feel trapped by them?

Or worse, what if everything fell apart on him? What if he was forced to sacrifice his life for her and the baby? She couldn't bear the thought of that. She loved him too much to be able to let that happen.

His broken dreams would break her heart, even if Duane never resented her. She'd hurt for him. He'd worked too long and too hard, believed he had so much to contribute to the state of Arizona. He needed his chance to make a difference.

And she needed a chance to live life feeling good about herself.

She would never convince Duane to let her go, but she was an independent woman who could take care of herself. She could take care of a situation that was getting the best of both of them. She'd slip away and have her baby, and Duane could have his campaign and the life he so obviously needed.

When the baby was born, she'd get in touch with him. He would know his child, even if the world didn't know the baby was his. More important, her child would know his father. That was a must.

Silent while the thoughts raced through her mind, Sophie hadn't noticed Sam finish his drink. Put down his glass. "I was thinking," he said, his voice low, coaxing. Too kind. "Maybe we could make a deal."

She wanted nothing from these people. "What kind of

deal?" What was Duane worth to his party? What was he getting himself into? Did he really want his campaign run by people like this? Was this the circle he moved in in the city? The type of life he lived?

"Well, now." Sam moved closer. "That really depends on you."

What!? "What are—"

He was too close.

Sophie raised her knee, hit out, but she'd realized too late where this was going. Sam easily captured her wrists and pressed his lips against hers.

CHAPTER TWENTY

JERKING HER HEAD TO the side, Sophie cried out. "Get off me!" She brought her knee up between them, pressing against the weight forcing her back into the soft leather. The hand that wasn't restraining her wrists ran across the underside of the hip she'd just exposed, and squeezed her bottom.

Sophie tried to scream.

But no sound came out.

She kicked. Gasped for air. She turned her head and tried to bring up her knee in a more strategic position, but he stopped her with one leg holding both of hers captive.

The six-foot, two-hundred-pound man was much bigger than she was. Much stronger.

"You're a fighter. That surprises me," he said. "But I'm game." Letting go of her hands, he circled her throat with his fingers, holding her head steady, and ground his lips against hers. Then, squeezing her jaw until she opened her mouth, he crammed his tongue down her throat.

Sophie choked, tears wetting her face as she tried to breathe.

He shifted, trapping her arms between their bodies, and she used them to hold his weight off her stomach, her breasts, to keep him at bay.

Her mind and heart were on the front door. *Come home, Duane. Help me!*

Livingston's hand moved down her throat to her chest and grabbed one of her breasts.

He squeezed. And squeezed again. "I wouldn't have thought Koch was a fighting man," he panted.

Oh, God, please help me.

She got a knee free, brought it up but missed her mark, cracking her kneecap on his tailbone.

She bit his wrist.

And saw stars when he backhanded her. Pain reverberated through her head. Her cheekbone and eye throbbed.

She was going to be beaten. Raped. Right here in her lover's upscale condominium.

"No!" Sophie tensed every muscle in her body—arms, legs, torso, anything that could press forward, force him off her.

"Hold it, bitch." Livingston pulled back, capturing her wrists on either side of her head, and restraining her body with the weight of his. His penis jutted against her pelvis and a part of her died.

Simply rolled over and turned out the light.

"Get off me, you bastard, or I swear to God I'll kill you." Her voice was soft. Deadly. Unrecognizable to her. "I'll charge your corpse with rape and sue your estate."

Not one more man was going to get away with mistreating her.

Ever.

Again.

Livingston froze. Stared at her. She could almost see the calculations going on inside his brain. And knew she'd won when the fingers digging into her wrists released enough to allow her blood to flow.

He held her still.

"Apparently I misread the situation," he said. "I thought we were willing participants. Playing a game."

Misread, my ass.

"I apologize if there's been some misunderstanding."

Had she been someone else, she might have laughed. Might have hit the man. Or called the police.

But she was Sophie Curtis. She had issues. A history. She was the secret lover of a powerful man. In his apartment. With one of his close associates. Also a powerful man.

She felt dirty. And hurt. And wanted to go home.

"Let go of me," she said through gritted teeth.

"I will," he said. "But—"

"Now." Her voice was a little stronger. A little louder.

Livingston let go of one of her wrists, but kept her in her seat. "Listen, I truly meant no harm. I thought we could come to an agreement. You know, whatever you're getting from Koch, I'll more than match. I'll take care of you. Protect you. You'll have a secure future. Just not with the man in the limelight."

"Let me go."

"Sure," he said, sitting back a bit. "But I have to tell you, this is the only offer you're going to get. And if you think you're going to play the innocent card, let me remind you that it'll be your word against mine and I've got twenty-five years in with the people of this town. They know my word is gold. Whereas you've got a past. A really messy, dirty past."

She was going to puke. And not because of the baby.

Her worst nightmare had come true.

SOPHIE DIDN'T SOUND HAPPY when Duane called her from his car on his way home Saturday afternoon. He didn't blame her. Her first day in town with him, her first day as his intended wife, and he'd left her alone for more than four hours.

And he was going to have to go out again.

It seemed that Tommy had hit his wife this time. Sort of. He'd pushed her away when she was trying to drag their two-year-old son out of Tommy's arms. He'd feared she intended to beat the boy for shaking his head at her. She'd tripped. She'd fallen backward. And required five stitches to close the gash on her head.

He'd been charged with domestic abuse.

Duane wasn't worried about the charge. They'd be able to beat that with self- and child-defense arguments. Right now what he cared about were those two little boys. With their father arrested, they'd been temporarily taken from his care. Duane had to get them back to him. He had two hours before he was set to appear before the commissioner to argue for his client.

Sophie wasn't waiting by the door as he'd hoped. He let himself in, taking the keys slowly out of the lock as he did a quick perusal of the room. It looked exactly as it had every other time he'd come over the past months. Pristine. Unoccupied.

"Soph?"

"Over here."

She was sitting in one of the home theater seats, hidden by the high back.

Not welcoming him home. Not kissing him in greeting. Not even saying hello.

Because he was late?

That wasn't like Sophie at all. Not even a changed Sophie, who had the confidence of knowing she was going to be his wife. A woman who now had the right to nag and have expectations.

"What's going on?" he asked, rounding the line of seats.

Then he saw her. Or rather, saw the swollen mark on her cheek, leading up to her eye.

He rushed over, dropped to his knees and scrutinized her for further damage. "My God! What happened?"

There wasn't any sign of a scuffle. Had she gone out? Wandered into a bad neighborhood? She wasn't in Shelter Valley anymore.

"I fell," she said, shrugging. "I put ice on it and it's fine. It looks a lot worse than it is."

She *fell?* "Where? How?"

"It's stupid," she said. "The tile was wet in the bathroom."

They'd gotten a little carried away in the shower. Quickly. Because he had to get to the jail.

"I slipped and caught the edge of my face on the vanity."

It was marble. They were lucky she hadn't broken the skin, needed stitches. Or worse.

"Does your head hurt?"

"Nope. Not at all. It's probably starting to wonder about its association with me, though. That's twice in a couple of days it's taken the rap for something I've done."

Something was wrong. Very wrong.

Had she decided, after hours of being trapped here, that she didn't want this kind of life, after all? Had she had too much time to think?

"Sophie?" Duane perched on the edge of the seat beside her, waited for her to look at him.

She didn't meet his gaze for a long time.

When she did, he'd never seen her look so lost. Or…broken.

"What's going on, babe? Talk to me."

"I…have something…to…tell…you." Each word seemed to require a new breath.

And when he reached out to gently touch her face, she winced.

So much for there being no pain. It wasn't merely swollen, either. There was a definite welt beneath the redness. She'd hit herself a lot harder than she'd said.

"Whatever it is, we'll deal with it," he said, refusing to give in to fear. "From now on, it's you and me, Soph." He held up her hand, turned it so that she could see the ring he'd given her. "Remember?"

As he was taking comfort from the fact that the diamond was indeed still on her finger, Sophie's eyes filled with tears. She shook her head.

And pulled off his ring.

"I can't wear this."

So it was worse than he'd thought. Her mind had managed to do quite a job on her during those solitary hours. She was out of her element. In completely unfamiliar surroundings. Her doubts were understandable.

Still, Sophie wasn't any small-town innocent. She'd traveled the country. Alone.

"Can't, or won't?" he asked, still holding her hand. He didn't take back the ring.

"Can't."

Get the facts, man. Then find the solution, the way to win. You know the drill.

"Why not?"

"I've…done something, Duane. Something horrible." She glanced down.

Staring at her bent head, he tried not to panic. To keep his thoughts focused. She was the case of a lifetime. She was his life. Something he should have realized months ago.

"You've only been here alone a few hours," he said, doing his damnedest to keep his voice light. He would have liked to manage a teasing tone, but that seemed too big of a stretch even for him. "What could you possibly have done?

His words may or may not have had an effect on her, but they calmed him. He'd only been gone a few hours. How bad could it be?

"Let me guess, you broke my Most Valuable Player trophy from college." Back then he'd had this idea that he was going to play professional baseball for California. But he'd been passed over for a couple of guys younger than he was. Guys who'd signed up before getting a college education. One of them had gone on to make millions.

And none of that had anything to do with the mother of his child, hunched here with his ring hanging off the end of her index finger. She sniffled, and he wanted to hug her to him and keep her safely against his heart forever.

Then she looked up. The resolute stare she gave him, her suddenly straightened spine, gave him no warning at all. "I slept with James Benson."

He heard the words. Even pictured the other man, dropping his bag of cookies on Sophie's front porch. Perching on a ladder by her back wall. Soothing the side of her head with an ice pack when she'd hurt herself.

"When?" he asked. Not because he cared, but because it seemed to be his job to do something about the silence that had fallen.

Nothing was making sense.

She'd hit her head. Twice. Was hurt worse than she'd said. Craziness was talking. She'd taken his ring the night before. She wouldn't have done that if—

Chilled to the bone, Duane remembered that she hadn't taken his ring. She'd said she wanted to. She'd said she loved him. She'd looked so longingly at what he was offering her.

He'd put the ring on her finger and taken her to bed.

She'd been going to tell him then, hadn't she?

No way. Life didn't happen this way except on television. On the shows he didn't watch. Or in the books he didn't read.

Except things did happen. He heard about it every single day of his life. In the office. In court. He made a living from the insane things people did to each other. People who loved each other.

Crazy. Two blows in two days had to have caused too much swelling of her brain. She was delusional. She'd dreamed the encounter. She was confused. He needed to get her to the hospital.

Then everything would be okay.

"I'm sorry, Duane." The tears she'd been seeming to fight dripped down her cheeks. "So, so sorry."

And that was that. Sophie stood, put his ring in the cup holder between them. She glanced at it once, then hurried toward the bedroom.

A nice, dramatic exit from a theater major. A young theater-production manager. He'd give her a minute, then he'd go to her. He'd make her tell him everything.

He'd make himself listen.

He'd find a way to make life right again. Find a way to make them right.

She must have missed that part in the script.

Before he'd moved from the chair, Sophie was back, her packed bag on her shoulder, along with the bag she carried as a purse.

"I'll be out of town after next week," she said. "If you wouldn't mind waiting, you can come pick up your stuff sometime while I'm gone. Just leave your key on the counter."

He heard the clink of light metal against granite—her key on his counter—then she was gone.

CHAPTER TWENTY-ONE

SOPHIE SOBBED for the first part of the journey home, until she realized her blurred vision was putting her baby's life in danger. She turned on the audio book she'd been listening to what seemed like weeks ago, but had only been before her last trip. She couldn't really remember the story, but focusing on the steady voice helped.

She went straight to her house. Living on the outskirts of town meant she could sneak in without anyone knowing she was home. She'd told Phyllis she was spending the weekend in Phoenix. No one would be checking on her, or paying her a visit. Pulling into her garage, she quickly shut the door. And planned to leave all of her lights off for the next twenty-four hours. At least.

She needed some time totally alone. Time to get herself under control. To come to grips with herself before anyone else started filling her head with well-meaning advice or commiseration.

She needed time to figure out the right thing to do.

But first, she needed time to fall apart.

Allowing the sobs to come as she unlocked her door, Sophie surprised herself by entering the kitchen dry-eyed. And the bedroom, as well.

From wherever the tears had sprung, they'd retreated.

She was on her own here. Plans, responsibilities, security and health were all up to her. But she wasn't a planner and provider for herself anymore. Someone else was dependent upon her.

She wasn't going to let her baby down.

In lieu of falling apart she cleaned. Herself first, scrubbing skin that the slime, Livingston, had never touched. And especially the places he had. When she'd run out of hot water in the shower, she threw away the clothes she'd been wearing, then got dressed.

The house was next. Everything she could find. Sinks. The shower. The spare bedroom closet. Everything had to have a purpose, or it was gone. She had no room in her life for superfluous hangers-on.

When her face started to throb, she put ice on it. When her cell phone rang, she ignored it.

And when she felt like she was going to throw up, she ate saltine crackers.

Noticing that she'd left the air compressor out in the yard two days before, she retrieved it.

And, too late, noticed the man picking oranges behind her.

"I talked to a few people in town this morning and have places to deliver the rest of these oranges," he called. "Hated to see them go to waste."

"Oh. Good." That should do it. Allow her to escape and be alone.

"I didn't notice any lights on over there last night."

His nosiness had now gone overboard. She had to put a stop to it. As soon as she found an ounce of spare energy to fight. "I was in Phoenix." And in case he'd misunderstood somewhere along the way that she was in a relationship—or had been until she'd appropriated him as her fake lover—she added, "With Duane."

James moved, slipped, and her head shot up. Only to see that he'd recovered himself and was staring at her.

He was over the wall before she had a chance to form a sentence.

Or issue an invitation.

He moved with force, but the fingers that touched her face were gentle. "What in the hell happened to you?"

"I fell." The lie had worked with Duane, and he was about as savvy as they came. "On slippery tile in the bathroom. Hit my face on the vanity."

"Like hell you did," James practically growled. "A vanity would have left a horizontal mark, not three vertical ones."

What was the guy, a CSI freak?

"He hit you." The controlled anger in the man's voice was not to be brushed off. She got that loud and clear.

"No, he didn't," Sophie said. She'd broken Duane's heart today. In an effort to save his life. And the life of their child. But she absolutely would not hurt him again. Period.

"I swear to you, James. I fell. Duane wasn't even home when this happened. He was at work helping get a client out of jail. You or anyone investigating could verify my story in a matter of minutes."

Duane was a kind man. A passionate man, a strong, caring one. He'd never, ever hit a woman. Any woman.

Sophie's actions today had been to save his reputation, dammit. She wasn't going to have it smeared in another, even uglier way.

"You've been crying," James said, but she could tell by the stern set of his jaw that he wasn't letting this matter go.

She pleaded her case for another five minutes, but he

was ready to call the police. So because she was sacrificing everything to protect Duane and her baby, she told James a version of the truth.

She told him about Duane's proposal, about the things his party chairperson had said. She left out only the part about her morning visitor, insisting that she really had fallen and smacked her face against the corner of the vanity. Livingston wasn't going to say anything unless she did. He'd be stupid to open his mouth unless it was to counter something she said. And she knew better than to try. He'd wanted her gone. She was gone. End of their story.

Nor did she tell James about using him as her scapegoat with Duane, saying only that she'd told him she'd been unfaithful as a way to set him free.

"And he believed you?" James asked.

"Duane seems to have a hard time understanding why someone as young and smart and beautiful as me would be interested in someone as over the hill as he is. His words, not mine."

"I can see his point on that one," James said. "Most girls your age are exploring life's opportunities. A forty-six-year-old man has already been around many of the learning curves."

She shrugged. "Maybe. I guess it depends on what road he's traveled. Duane might know more about laws and investments than I do, but I know more about living with heart. It's a give and take. Besides, I don't love him for what he knows. I love him because of who he is."

Hands on his hips, James gave her a pointed glance. "Then why aren't you out there fighting for the two of you?"

"Because I'm pregnant."

DUANE WENT BACK TO WORK. Because that's what he did—what he could rely on. He got those little boys back to their father before bedtime.

He wasn't ready for his own bed, however. He did something he'd never done before. He drove to the condo, parked his car, then walked the few blocks to Mill Avenue—the party street for students of Arizona State University. He found an underground dueling pianos bar, an out-of-the-way table, and sat there to drink until they closed. At which time he meandered toward home, making it as far as the lake, where he decided to sit and contemplate life. The lake offered no answers, but it did soothe and quiet his mind, his soul.

He woke just before dawn, still dressed in his suit from the day before, his tie loosened and slightly skewed.

Muscles aching from sleeping on the ground and his head pounding from overindulgence, he rose, then went home to bed.

SOPHIE COULDN'T REMEMBER going to bed. One minute she and James had been sitting in her living room—he'd insisted on waiting on her hand and foot because she'd thrown up the dinner he'd made, and because she had a little bit of a headache—and the next thing she knew she was awake, fully dressed on her bed, with a spare blanket thrown over her. The sun was starting to rise.

She must have fallen asleep. And he'd carried her in.

The perfect opportunity to undress her, if ever there was one. And he hadn't done so. In a twenty-four-hour period she'd had a run-in with the worst type of man. And the best.

Thoughts of the day before had her shivering and off the bed.

She needed coffee. Even before a shower. She stumbled out to the kitchen to make some. And screamed at the sight of a body on her couch. A male body.

He sat up and she recognized the messy-haired, yawning man as her neighbor.

He'd slept over? To take care of her?

Or because now he'd ask for payment for his kindness? Did he think they were building something here?

That he'd be next?

"What are you doing here?" she demanded. Her frying pan was only steps away. And the butcher knife was there, too. No way was she going to be touched again. She was not going to be vulnerable. Or weak. Or used.

"Watching over you."

"I've been watching over myself for most of my life," she said, feeling not one ounce of gratitude for the time or effort he'd spent on her behalf.

Her couch wasn't all that comfortable as a bed—she'd tried it out once or twice.

"Then it's time you had someone give you a helping hand."

"I have as many helping hands as I need." She didn't budge. Still had the iron pan, within two steps. "I live in Shelter Valley, remember? If any of my friends knew I was in town, they'd have come over. I didn't want them here. I wanted to be alone."

Too late she realized what she'd said. She'd told him no one knew she was home. No one would be stopping by, or looking for her.

She'd sneaked into town. Hid her car behind her closed garage door.

Was she the dumbest woman on the face of this earth? Would she never learn?

Or did she have some kind of subconscious, self-destructive bent? Some need to hurt herself by putting herself in vulnerable positions with men?

"I'm not going to hurt you, Sophie." James hadn't moved. Nor had his voice lost the patient kindness with which he'd treated her since their very first meeting.

His gentle tone plus the sight of his hair sticking up on end calmed her a bit, comforted her. But not enough to move her away from her kitchen arsenal.

"I never said you were going to." How would she get rid of him? For good. This was too much. He was a virtual stranger and he'd come to her rescue twice now.

He'd spent the night in her home.

If Duane could see them, she'd never be able to convince him they hadn't slept together.

Did she ever intend to do so?

"You're a smart, strong woman who's had a few too many bumps along the way," James said. "And now, especially with the baby coming…I want to help you where I can. No strings attached."

Help her. Just help her. Even after all her years in Shelter Valley, her honorary position in the Sheffield family, the concept of someone only wanting to be nice to her was a hard one to grasp.

Because she was tired, and too confused with life to make sense of this stranger in her living room, she blurted out the sole question pounding in her brain. "Why?"

He looked as though he was going to speak, then didn't.

He sighed. "You deserve the truth."

His reply didn't do much to comfort her. "I want the truth."

"You're probably not going to like it," he said. "I'd appreciate a chance to use the restroom before we go any further. Do you mind?"

They weren't going any further. He was going to say what he had to say and be gone.

But if he was out of the room for a few moments, she could arm herself. And call Phyllis to ask her to phone back in fifteen minutes, then come to Sophie's rescue if she didn't answer.

Which was exactly what she did. After hauling her out of bed, she assured her friend that she was fine, that she was in the middle of an experiment, and she'd explain when Phyllis called back.

An experiment. Whether or not she could trust her instincts where a man was concerned. Or herself to take care of herself. Either way.

She heard the toilet flush, and her fingers tensed along the handle of the knife hidden beneath her shirt and the arms she'd wrapped around her middle. Water ran. He had ten minutes left before Phyllis phoned.

Then James was back. Pants fully zipped. Shirt tucked in. Shoes still on. His hair was no longer standing up.

She missed the look.

"Do you mind if we have a seat?" he asked, pointing to opposite ends of the kitchen table.

Not the couch. This one was either a strange breed, or really, really good at lulling his prey into a false sense of security.

She sat. Mostly because it was easier to conceal her knife under the table.

"I'm going to tell you something, Sophie," he said softly, looking at his hands folded in front of him as much as at her. "Though I promised myself I wouldn't, I find that some promises, especially those made without being in full possession of facts, have to be broken."

Okay, already. Get on with it. He had only seven minutes left.

"But I want you to make a promise that you will keep."

She didn't owe him anything. And didn't have time to play games, either. Six minutes. "What?"

"I want you to promise that when you hear what I have to say, you'll at least give me a chance to fully explain."

That was fair. James was a fair man. He'd been good to her. Before today, she'd actually liked him.

He'd spent all night in her home without trying to cuddle her in her sleep. Hadn't even loosened the top button of her blouse when he'd carried her to bed. Or used the excuse of staying close by in case of emergency to lie next to her instead of on a couch that was too narrow and too short to make a decent bed.

She only had five minutes left.

"Okay. I promise."

"I wish there was an easy way to break this to you, but there isn't."

He was really struggling. Emotionally distressed. James who, to this point, had been so strong, composed. So sure. So unmoved by everything.

"Just say it."

His long stare made her uncomfortable, as did the sadness she read in his eyes. Then he nodded. He spoke. She saw his lips move.

And seconds later, her brain translated the movement into sound. Into words.

"I'm your father."

THERE WAS A BANG on the door. Sophie heard it. Jumped. But continued to stare at the man watching her from the other end of the table.

"This is the sheriff, open up!"

That got her attention enough for her to glance at the front door. And to watch as James Benson—her *father?*—walked slowly to the door, opened it with one hand above his head and quickly raised the other.

She was beside him then, somehow, pushing herself slightly in front of him. "Don't shoot, Greg. He's my dad."

At which time she noticed Phyllis and Matt right behind Greg, and the world started to spin. Then, as two sets of male arms tangled around her body, supporting her, everything went black.

CHAPTER TWENTY-TWO

IF THE DAMN PHONE DIDN'T quit ringing he was going to pull the cord out of the wall.

It rang again. Duane swatted at a space beside the bed. And swatted again. Two rings later, he remembered he no longer had a landline at home. He'd opened one eye to check.

Another peal. His cell phone was ringing.

What time was it?

Not sure he could roll over with the thickness wrapped around his head, Duane tried to see enough of the clock to get even a hint of some logistical bearings.

The thought, the very effort, hurt.

But the ringing stopped. Finally. A few seconds without sound. He could go back to sleep. And figure out the time when he woke up.

Riiinnnggg.

He was having a nightmare. The phone could not be ringing again. But the agonizing sharpness searing his brain forced him to accept that he was going to have to move. It was either that or suffer death by ringing.

He caught a one-eyed glimpse of the clock on the nightstand as he stumbled past to find his cell phone.

Nine. In the morning, he assumed, based on the brightness he was trying to avoid by walking with his eyes shut.

Sunday morning, he hoped. If it was Monday he was going to have some explaining to do.

Especially to himself.

What in the hell had he done? He knew better than this.

And where was the damn phone?

When he tripped over the jacket lying in the middle of the marble floor between his foyer and his living room, he was almost glad to go down. Glad to be able to rest his head for another moment.

Until the sound started again. He'd found his phone right beneath his head.

Groaning, closer to tears than he wanted to admit, Duane hauled himself to his feet. He'd done this to himself. After drinking so much, he deserved to suffer. Needed to suffer. Lest he ever get the bright idea to take himself off on another irresponsible binge.

Forty-five minutes, three cups of coffee, a spell over the commode and a shower later, Duane once again heard his phone. This time he was sober enough to realize that there must be a problem if someone was trying so hard to reach him on a Sunday morning.

From there, he thought of Sophie. And ran. If anything had happened to her...

"What?" he barked into the mouthpiece, without taking the time to see who was calling.

"It's Will." The words instilled more panic in Duane's rapidly pounding heart.

"Will? What's wrong? Has something happened to Sophie?"

"It's not Sophie I'm calling about," Will said, his words odd. His voice odd. Duane's half-sloshed brain wasn't thinking fast enough to figure out anything beyond that impressive observation. He could remember hearing Will so exhausted, so disheartened only one other time. When Becca had asked him for a separation.

"If not about Sophie, then what?" Duane asked. Was it Will and Becca again? Duane would never have believed it possible.

"I take it you haven't seen the morning paper?"

The morning paper? Did that mean Sophie was all right? And that Will and Becca and their kids were, too?

"No, I'm taking it slow this morning," Duane said.

"Listen, Duane, I'm not good at this," Will said. "Get a paper, and meet me at the Valley Diner at noon." Opening time on Sunday.

"I'm in Phoenix," Duane explained, wondering what had happened to his friend. Will had to be in some kind of trouble.

"I know. Just get here."

If Will was in trouble, Duane would travel to the moon if need be to help him.

"I'm on my way."

DUANE DIDN'T MAKE IT past the lobby without stopping.

As he approached the paper stand, digging in his pocket for change, Walt, the doorman, called out to him. "Hey, isn't that the young lady you brought in here Friday night?" He was pointing to the stand.

Focusing on the newsprint behind the locked bars that prevented anyone from stealing a paper, Duane started to shake when he saw Sophie's picture staring back at him. It was an old one, probably taking during her college days—maybe even lifted from a yearbook? Her hair was longer. And her eyes—they were younger, too. Wilder. And empty.

It took him two tries to get the blasted box open, and when he did, he was afraid he was going to be sick a second time.

Young Gold Digger Double Dips.

He didn't know what the hell that meant.

But he was damn certain he was going to find out.

And kill whoever had done this to her.

SOPHIE WASN'T LEFT ALONE, even for a second, the rest of that morning. Phyllis stayed with her while James left to shower and Matt went home to relieve Tory of the twins, get them dressed and fed before bringing them to Sophie's house.

Tory stopped by to see her before Matt returned.

"So I was right," Tory said. "You've won your fight against bulimia just like you thought."

Sophie and Phyllis shared a grin. "Yep."

Grabbing Sophie's hand, Tory sat beside her on the couch—the only place Sophie was allowed to be right now other than the bathroom.

"So, we'll do this one together, huh?" she asked, glancing at Sophie's tummy.

Embarrassed, shy all of a sudden, Sophie nodded. And teared up again. "I don't know what in the hell's the matter with me," she said. "Everything's making me cry."

"Might be because in twenty-four hours you lied to the man you love, found out he didn't trust you when he believed your outrageous fib, you've hit your head—twice—and met your father." Phyllis's expression matched her wry tone of voice.

"And you're pregnant," Tory said. "Hormones, honey. Crying happens."

"Sophie Curtis, you lied to me!" James's deep voice bellowed from the back door, right before the screen almost came off its hinges with the force of his thrust. The man was pissed. "I've already called Greg Richards and we're going to press charges against this guy. Right after you tell us what really happened to you yesterday."

"Hey." Phyllis stood, Tory right beside her, facing James, her hands on her hips. "No matter who you say you are, buster, Sophie doesn't need—"

"Wait." Sophie stood, too. And suffered no dizziness at all. She was pregnant, not sick. All this pampering had to stop.

Apparently eight long years of fighting bulimia hadn't taught her a thing. She didn't know how James had found out, but she was ashamed that he had. All his talk about her being independent, capable, and yesterday she'd fallen right back into the trap that had been set for her, seemingly, at birth.

Taking the blame. Keeping quiet. Hiding. Accepting abuse. Realizing all eyes were trained on her, she glared at the man who'd just come bellowing into her house, and said the first thing that came to her mind.

"Where were you after I turned two?" Before he could respond, she added, "And when I wrote to you in high school?" Okay, maybe that one wasn't completely fair— her mother had given her a fake name and address. "Where were you when that bastard brushed my breasts every chance he got?" Yeah, there were other issues here. More recent ones. But maybe she had a lot of wrongs to right.

James didn't shrink as three sets of eyes turned on him. His own eyes filled with moisture instead.

"I didn't leave your mother when you were two, Soph," he said softly, with so much love in his voice she wanted to hate him. She didn't need this now. She'd needed it twenty-eight years ago. And twenty-seven. And twenty-six…

"I told you what happened in my life. The only part I left out was a most recent development."

She remembered the other day on his porch. His story about a wife he'd adored. A big-time job for a kid high on life. An avaricious receptionist...

If it was true, then...

"The receptionist. That was my mother?" Sophie had never once heard her mention working at such a menial job. Even for a day.

James nodded. "But I didn't know that until about six months ago. Apparently husband number six, or seven—I can't remember what she said—left her, and she's not as young as she used to be. The sags are starting to become more obvious. Or the surgery is. In any case, she tried to reel me in a second time and when that failed, she told me I'd had a child all those years ago. Told me that she'd make the information public if I didn't agree to pay her back monthly support for the first eighteen years of your life."

Sophie sat abruptly. Phyllis and Tory sank, too, one on each side of her. She hadn't spoken to her mom in a few years. But apparently the woman had not softened.

"So you agreed?" Sophie asked.

"Hell no! I had her charged with a bribery attempt, and hired a detective to find you. Then I had an attorney negotiate with the people who'd rented the house behind you for the winter so that I could have it instead."

"Were you still in Denver?" As far as she knew her mother had never lived anyplace else. "Or ever in Denver?"

He nodded, the sadness returning to his eyes. "When I think of all the years we missed, the life we could have had, the things I had a right to share with you and the suffering you've experienced because of not having a father—"

"You'll make yourself crazy, James." Phyllis's soft inter-jection stopped the flow of regret. It would always exist, but could ruin their lives if they let it.

"She's right," Tory said. "I learned that one the hard way. I almost lost my husband due to my inability to let go of past regret."

"And I'll never have a chance at a healthy life if I can't let go of that," Sophie added, her smile tentative as she looked at the man she'd thought was a nice guy. A kind friend.

Odd, how awkward she felt around James now. He was her father. Flesh of her flesh. She had his genes inside of her and—

"Oh my gosh!" she said aloud, staring straight at the man. "You're going to be a grandfather!"

COLLEGE COED GRADUATES to the Big Time. Duane made himself look at the paper again as he sat in his Mercedes, still parked in his garage, with his keys in his lap. The subhead was no better than the lead-in. And the article was worse.

Entrepreneur, well-known philanthropist and last living son of an old-money Boston family, turned Scottsdale elitist, Sam Livingston had visited his condo yesterday.

"I can sure understand how Koch was hoodwinked by the filly," Livingston was quoted as saying. "That good man wanted to marry her. To make an honest woman of her. But there are some women who just don't fit well in married life."

Livingston went on to accuse Sophie of first coming on to him, offering to "care" for him in exchange for his "caring" for her. According to him, he'd refused, of course. The article went on to state that while Koch couldn't be reached for comment, party officials had extended their sympathy and support to him.

"Bullshit!" Duane spat as he threw the paper. His first thought was to drive to Scottsdale, haul Samuel P. Livingston off his several-million-dollar estate and beat him to a pulp.

Duane's second was to get to Shelter Valley, to Sophie, as quickly as the Mercedes could safely take him.

Words he hadn't even known he knew spewed from his lips as he headed out of town. They didn't accomplish much. Except, perhaps, keep him on the road. Exactly what had the man done to her?

Duane thought of the swelling on Sophie's face. No big deal, she'd said. A fall against the vanity.

He should have known.

Damn Livingston. Duane brushed at his blurry eyes as he pushed the pedal to the floor and drove through the desert.

If he'd raped her, Livingston would pay. Duane knew some people, too. The attorney general, for one. The county attorney for another.

He'd see that charges were pressed and the case won— one way or another.

But how he'd ever make this up to the woman he loved, he had no idea.

CHAPTER TWENTY-THREE

SOPHIE WAS IN THE living room with her father and Phyllis—Tory having gone home to her family—when Matt returned. Without the twins.

"Where are Clarissa and Calvin?" Sophie asked. She needed a dose of their innocence. A break from the pressure she was getting from her team of self-appointed caregivers.

"With the Parsonses," Matt said, his face grim. The newspaper sticking out from under his arm said it all.

Shaking his head, sending Sophie a look that was a mix of protectiveness and sympathy, he threw the paper on the coffee table where everyone could read it at once.

"We've seen this." James picked up the newspaper, ripped it in half and threw it in the trash.

They'd spent the past ten minutes trying to convince Sophie that whether Sam Livingston had the power of God or not, she could stand up to him.

When James came back and joined the rest of them in the living room, he looked straight at Sophie. "You're going to talk to Greg."

Sophie nodded. In that moment, she knew something else, too. The days of her having to figure out all alone what to do were gone.

Forever.

MATT ANSWERED THE DOOR when Duane knocked. Considering the circumstances of Sophie's departure the day before, he'd decided not to use his key.

"Hi," he said. "I need to see Sophie." He'd skipped his meeting with Will, having already figured out what it would have been about. His friend would understand.

"I'm sorry," Matt said, blocking the doorway. "She's not taking visitors right now."

"Cut the crap, Matt. I'm not a visitor and you know it."

"She doesn't want to see anyone."

It took Duane a couple of seconds to realize that Matt was completely serious.

"She has to see me," Duane said. She was in love with him. Or had been before he'd left her alone and helpless in unfamiliar surroundings. Until he'd left her exposed and defenseless. "I love her, Matt. Please. I need to talk to her."

To his credit, Matt faltered for a moment, then shook his head. "Maybe in another day or two."

"Tell her it's me," he said, willing to beg if that's what it took. "She'll see me if she knows I'm here."

"She knows, man," Matt finally said. "She saw your car out front."

"And she won't see me."

"No."

"But—"

"Emphatically, no, Duane. She said she'd call the sheriff if you didn't go peacefully."

Recognizing that he had to leave, that he was only going to make things worse, uglier, for Sophie if he persisted, Duane turned. But he had no idea where to go. What to do.

He'd thought his life was in Phoenix. In politics. He'd found out too late it had been right here in Shelter Valley all along.

"I KNOW I SHOULDN'T HAVE lied," Sophie told the small audience sitting with her. The Sheffields, who'd literally saved her life, and the man who'd given her life. "I should have told Duane that Livingston had been there, should have told him what really happened. But don't you see?" She looked from one to another. "There was no way to fix this one. It didn't matter what we told the press, people will always believe the worst. Even his own people believe it, so how could we hope to convince those who don't have any personal stake in Duane's life?"

The nods she received didn't give her any peace.

"If it had just been me," she said, repeating what she'd told James the night before, "I might have chanced it. But with the baby…"

"Duane would have stood by you." Matt had been a lot quieter since his trip to the door half an hour before.

"Yes, and at what cost? And at what cost to our child? Bad enough that I was a gold digger, but one who used the oldest trick in the book to trap a man? What would that do to Duane's future chances of winning an election? How could people trust him if he could get trapped that way? He might as well drop his name from the ballot right here and now."

"Which is Duane's choice to make," Phyllis said.

"I know. But I'm still not sure I'd be making the best choice by marrying him."

"You're in love with him." Phyllis again.

"Yes."

"He's obviously in love with you," Matt said.

"What's holding you back?" James asked. "Just his career? Your fear of ending his dreams? Because I can tell you, they're empty if you don't have the woman you love beside you, sharing the victories with you. And no number of goals met, no amount of money, will ever compensate for missing the growing years of your child."

"Duane is as guilty as the rest of them." There. Sophie had said it out loud. Admitted to herself, and to her family, the truth about the man she loved.

"What?" Phyllis was the one who spoke, but all three sets of eyes held the question.

"He believed me yesterday when I told him I'd slept with someone else. You see, Duane thinks I'm incapable of knowing the difference between right and wrong. He doesn't blame me for it. He knows that my perceptions were skewed because of my upbringing. But he still thinks it. Obviously, today, he's seen the light or he wouldn't have come here. Maybe the paper did it. Maybe, because he saw my bruise, he put two and two together. But the problem is another time, another circumstance, when a man comes on to me, if I'm friendly back, he's going to start thinking things again."

"So yesterday was a test," James said.

Sophie was flooded with a weird kind of Christmas-present magic every time she looked at the man. Odd, considering that the rest of her heart was shattered in little pieces. "What do you mean?"

"Yesterday, when you told him you slept with someone else. If he'd said he didn't believe you, you would have stayed."

Would she have? She didn't think so. There was still the baby to consider. His political career. The press…

Would she have?

She had a flashback to earlier that day. She hadn't wanted Duane to see James in her home because then she would never have the chance to convince him she hadn't slept with her neighbor. Although she was pretty sick about the fact that she'd used James's name, now that she knew who he was.

"I don't know," she finally said. "But the fact is, he did believe me."

HE COULDN'T LEAVE TOWN. He probably should. But Sophie was here. His heart was here. There was simply no place else to go.

Duane drove by the diner. Will's car was out front. Duane had no idea what to do, no clear goal. So he parked and watched as people came and went. A few of them he recognized. Most of them, not. Because this was Sophie's town. Her people. He'd clung to his own identity. Phoenix. Surface relationships.

With a clarity Duane would have given anything to have had even one day earlier, he saw himself: a man who'd consciously chosen the circle he'd joined, consciously chosen and tended to his associations. Sure Sophie had done the same for herself. But she'd been far wiser than him in the making of those choices. She'd surrounded herself with good people who cared deeply for her.

And he was the one who was supposed to have all the experience? The one who was being "used" by the gold digger to "save" her? Save her from what? Heaven? A town full of people who were protecting her, loving her, caring for her, where he'd failed?

Looking around at the stores closed in observance of the day of rest, Duane felt as though he was seeing them for the first time. As though he was discovering the great secret of life. Families and friends smiled and waved as they passed each other on the street. He looked toward the park in the center of town, with the statue of the original Sam Montford, who'd founded Shelter Valley. He, a white man, had married the love of his life. A black woman. His people—privileged, rich, powerful people—hadn't approved. After losing his wife to the brutality of an unaccepting society, he'd settled in Shelter Valley to build a home, and a life, that he could endure. A life, a small world, based on basic principles he'd learned along the way. Principles like loyalty, kindness and acceptance.

Acceptance.

That's all Sophie had wanted and needed. All she'd ever asked for. Money and power didn't matter to her. She just wanted to love and be loved. So simple. Yet, apparently for him, the hardest thing of all to understand.

After ten minutes of sitting, Duane got out of the car and, squaring his shoulders, went into the diner. He wasn't one of them. He didn't deserve their understanding or acceptance. He simply had no place else to be.

No place he wanted to be.

"You didn't disappoint me." Will's words of greeting surprised Duane as he slid into the other side of the booth.

"How so?" He wasn't equipped for mind games or wordplay.

Indicating his cell phone on the table, Will said, "They called to say you'd gone to Sophie's. I was pretty sure this would be your next stop."

"So you waited."

"Obviously." The eggs on the plate in front of Will turned Duane's stomach. When the waitress came by, he asked for a cup of coffee and dry toast.

"I have to see her, Will."

"I know you think you do."

"I *do*."

"Like I knew I had to see Becca some nine years ago and you, over a game of cards, talked to me about divorce instead."

"I was an ass."

"You were ignorant."

Maybe a kinder way of saying the same thing.

"I'm not ignorant today," he said. "Look, Will, I'm forty-six years old. It's taken me half a lifetime to discover what living even is. I have no excuses for that. But I love Sophie. And I believe she loves me. I have no idea why but I finally get that in all the world, I'm the one who touches that amazing woman's heart. And she's most certainly the only one who's ever touched mine. Hell, I'm risking everything, throwing away every goal I've ever had, to be with her. And I'm not going to abandon her. You can set up your block-ades and do whatever else it is you do in this town to protect your own, but I'm not going away. I *can* make her happy. And I won't give up trying until the day I die."

Will's slow smile was a bit discordant with the moment. "You've figured it out," he said, sounding far too pleased for a man who was spending his Sunday noon with a repro-bate friend in a sordid mess.

"What?"

"That, in the end, the only thing worth having, the only thing worth fighting for, is love. Life is guaranteed to give you challenges and temptations and confusions, but if you can come back to the love, every time, you will live a far happier life."

Happier. An odd concept to a man who'd always defined life in terms of success. Because he'd thought success meant happiness? Or because he'd never looked any further than success? Success was something he could obtain by hard work and effort. Something he could control.

"I need your help. I have to see her, Will. Please."

Will stared at him for an uncomfortably long moment. Then picked up his cell phone. "I'll see what I can do."

CHAPTER TWENTY-FOUR

SHAKING INSIDE AND OUT, Duane stepped up to Sophie's porch for the second time that day. At least the Sheffields' car was gone. He was going to have the love of his life to himself. For the few minutes she'd see him, anyway.

It probably wasn't going to happen today, but he was going to get her back. If it took months of courting her, years even, he was going to show her she could trust him to love her. And love her right. To trust her. And to put her first.

The pep talk didn't stop the clench of nerves in his gut when he heard the lock turn. The door opened and he straightened to face…James Benson.

"I'm here to see Sophie."

"I know." The other man nodded. "Come in. She's in the living room."

Trembling with more than nerves now, Duane approached the room slowly. Sophie was sitting on the couch, a green throw pillow hugged to her stomach. They'd picked those pillows out together. On the Internet. Because they didn't go out to shopping malls together.

She looked pale.

"Oh God, Soph." He couldn't help but hurry to her when he saw the bruise that engulfed most of one side of her face. "I'm so sorry, baby. So sorry. You should have told me. I—"

"Excuse me." Benson spoke from behind him. "I'm going to slip over to my place for a few minutes. I'll be back." He was talking to Sophie.

But Duane stood and faced him. "I appreciate the fact that you've been kind to Sophie," he said, with no fight left in him. "She speaks highly of you and I hope we can get to know each other better in the future." He should have been surprised to find that he meant those words, but after all that had happened in the past twenty-four hours, he wasn't. Duane Koch had been humbled. And the experience wasn't nearly as bad as he'd imagined it could be.

"But I also need you to know that I'm in love with her," he continued. A man could only take so much. "I believe she's in love with me. And I'm not leaving here until she's agreed to put my ring back on her finger and keep it there."

"That's up to her, don't you think?" James had a confidence Duane envied.

"Excuse me!" Sophie stood. "I'm right here, gentlemen. And can speak for myself."

She looked at Duane. "I told you yesterday, I—"

"Slept with James. Yes, I know." He was only allowed to stay until she asked him to leave, and might not have much time. "But we both know that wasn't true," he said, needing to get through the superfluous stuff so he could reach the part where she put his ring back on. "I couldn't figure out yesterday why you said it, other than to get yourself out of our relationship. I wasn't sure why, all of a sudden, you'd felt so threatened you had to resort to lying. This morning I knew."

For the first time since he'd come in, Sophie's expression faltered. "You knew?"

"That you were lying?"

She nodded.

"Of course I knew, Soph." He lowered his voice, automatically, and not because the other man was in the room. "I'm jealous, I'm not stupid. How can I love you and think, for one second, that you'd be disloyal to me? You couldn't do that to yourself."

"But…" She frowned. "You said…you think I might go elsewhere—"

"I'm forty-six years old, sweetie. I was caught up with the idea that you might tire of me. But I never thought you'd be unfaithful to me. What I feared was that I'd come home someday to find you there, waiting to tell me that you had to move on. Because you have an entire world to move on to. It wasn't your morals I was questioning, Soph. It was my allure."

James cleared his throat. "I think, before this goes much further—"

"Yes." Duane didn't take his eyes off Sophie. "Could you excuse us?"

"Um, Duane?" Her tentative smile was a bit crooked due to the swelling on her face. "Actually, since you have my ring, you really should speak to him about marrying me before he goes. It'd be kind of a shame to have to bring him back later and interrupt…things." She was grinning fully now, though her voice was shaking. She had tears in her eyes, too.

"Speak to James…?"

"Yes." With a wink at Sophie, James stepped up. "It's customary, I believe, for a man to ask a girl's father for her hand in marriage, is it not?"

"Her…" Duane's head was spinning now. "Did you say father?"

"Yes." This time, when Sophie walked over to the other

man, put her arm around his waist and smiled up at him, Duane could only stare. "Duane, meet my father, James Benson. Daddy, this is Duane."

"IT'S A LITTLE ODD, having a father-in-law who's only eight years older than I am."

Sitting next to Duane on the couch, holding his hand, Sophie nodded, but felt no threat, or fear, now as she considered their situation. It was odd. A fact of life. And nothing else.

"Yeah, kind of odd having a dad, after twenty-eight years without one, too." Her father had just left for the second time, having returned to have a late lunch with her and Duane. The two men had discussed Duane's political ambitions, and Duane had accepted James's avowal to help where he could, if Duane still wanted to pursue a life of service.

To Sophie's surprise, the love of her life had then said that, while he was sure he could make a difference, he wasn't certain that politics was the only way to do so. He'd said he and Sophie would talk about it and make their decision together. Sophie figured if they managed to get over their hurdles, they'd find a way to help Duane fulfill his goals. He was driven for a reason. The public needed him.

But so did she.

He shifted and, too late, she realized he'd reached into the pocket of his pants.

"Please marry me, Sophie," he said, holding out the ring she'd been afraid she'd never see again.

She took it this time. But she didn't put it on.

Because just as she'd learned much about herself over the past few days, she'd also learned much about the man she loved. Duane might be almost two decades older than her, but in life, they were in exactly the same place. Afraid of being alone. And afraid to love. Afraid because once you believed, you'd never, ever be able to settle for less again. Which made you vulnerable.

Something neither she nor Duane were any good at.

"You don't have to do this. Not until you're really comfortable with it. Not until you're ready."

"Oh, yes, I do have to do this." His reply brooked no argument whatsoever. "I don't think I can face another day not knowing that we're tied to each other. Yesterday wouldn't have happened if you'd had my openly stated protection. And, by the way, we're going to talk about that. I want to hear every detail of every second that bastard was in our home. And together we're going to get him. I've already made a couple of calls to press charges."

She didn't want to think about that now, to feel bad when she was feeling so good. "My father has already been all over me about pressing charges," she admitted. "Greg Richards is going to stop by tonight to take a deposition here, and he offered to go with me to the Tempe police."

"I'll go with you." There was no doubt that Duane was going to be the man protecting her from that point on if she'd let him. And Sophie figured she would. It might not be real independent and strong of her, but she allowed herself to like the feeling.

Because now she knew that being cared for didn't make her weak or helpless. Being cared for meant she had someone to take care of.

"So…" Duane nodded. "About that ring."

"I don't know, Duane." What was the matter with her? "I just… Once I put that on, I'm never going to be able to take it off. Maybe we should wait until you're sure how you feel about me. Sure that you can be happy with me even if it means you don't win the election."

"Sophie, I love you. More than that, I'm *in* love with you. It's taken me a long time to fall, but I'm not a stupid man. I know better than to walk away from my only chance at happiness when it sits down next to me on a bar stool. Don't you get that?"

Her entire body flooded with warmth. Sexual and otherwise. "I'm starting to."

"It's my fault that you don't already," he said. "Because I didn't understand how it all worked myself, until recently. I didn't distinguish the difference between happiness and success. Happiness and satisfaction. You're happiness. At best, politics would be success and satisfaction. I also didn't get that there has to be a pyramid, of sorts, with your partner always at the top, and everything else layered by level of importance underneath it."

Such a logical, Duane way of describing love. And so true.

"I'm sorry it took me so long, Soph. Sorry for being so dense. I promise you I will spend the rest of my life making it up to you."

"And I promise to love you, Duane, with my whole heart, my whole body, my whole soul."

He kissed her, and Sophie, wrapped in his arms, had not one single doubt left. About herself. Or about him.

"Now about that ring. Put it on, Soph. Give my heart some peace. Please?"

Give my heart some peace. She loved the sound of that. And as she slid the symbol of their promises to each other onto her finger, Sophie found out what a peaceful heart felt like.

* * * * *

*Celebrate 60 years of pure
reading pleasure with Harlequin®!
Silhouette® Romantic Suspense is celebrating
with the glamour-filled, adrenaline-charged
series* LOVE IN 60 SECONDS
*starting in April 2009.
Six stories that promise to bring
the glitz of Las Vegas, the danger of revenge,
the mystery of a missing diamond, family scandals
and ripped-from-the-headlines intrigue.
Get your heart racing as
love happens in sixty seconds!*

Enjoy a sneak peek of
USA TODAY *bestselling author
Marie Ferrarella's
THE HEIRESS'S 2-WEEK AFFAIR
Available April 2009
from Silhouette® Romantic Suspense.*

Eight years ago Matt Shaffer had vanished out of Natalie Rothchild's life, leaving behind a one-line note tucked under a pillow that had grown cold: *I'm sorry, but this just isn't going to work.*

That was it. No explanation, no real indication of remorse. The note had been as clinical and compassionless as an eviction notice, which, in effect, it had been, Natalie thought as she navigated through the morning traffic. Matt had written the note to evict her from his life.

She'd spent the next two weeks crying, breaking down without warning as she walked down the street, or as she sat staring at a meal she couldn't bring herself to eat.

Candace, she remembered with a bittersweet pang, had tried to get her to go clubbing in order to get her to forget about Matt.

She'd turned her twin down, but she did get her act

together. If Matt didn't think enough of their relationship to try to contact her, to try to make her understand why he'd changed so radically from lover to stranger, then to hell with him. He was dead to her, she resolved. And he'd remained that way.

Until twenty minutes ago.

The adrenaline in her veins kept mounting.

Natalie focused on her driving. Vegas in the daylight wasn't nearly as alluring, as magical and glitzy as it was after dark. Like an aging woman best seen in soft lighting, Vegas's imperfections were all visible in the daylight. Natalie supposed that was why people like her sister didn't like to get up until noon. They lived for the night.

Except that Candace could no longer do that.

The thought brought a fresh, sharp ache with it.

"Damn it, Candy, what a waste," Natalie murmured under her breath.

She pulled up before the Janus casino. One of the three valets currently on duty came to life and made a beeline for her vehicle.

"Welcome to the Janus," the young attendant said cheerfully as he opened her door with a flourish.

"We'll see," she replied solemnly.

As he pulled away with her car, Natalie looked up at the casino's logo. Janus was the Roman god with two faces, one pointed toward the past, the other facing the future. It struck her as rather ironic, given what she was doing here, seeking out someone from her past in order to get answers so that the future could be settled.

The moment she entered the casino, the Vegas phenomena took hold. It was like stepping into a world where time did not matter or even make an appearance. There was only a sense of "now."

Because in Natalie's experience she'd discovered that bartenders knew the inner workings of any establishment they worked for better than anyone else, she made her way to the first bar she saw within the casino.

The bartender in attendance was a gregarious man in his early forties. He had a quick, sexy smile, which was probably one of the main reasons he'd been hired. His name tag identified him as Kevin.

Moving to her end of the bar, Kevin asked, "What'll it be, pretty lady?"

"Information." She saw a dubious look cross his brow. To counter that, she took out her badge. Granted she wasn't here in an official capacity, but Kevin didn't need to know that. "Were you on duty last night?"

Kevin began to wipe the gleaming black surface of the bar. "You mean during the gala?"

"Yes."

The smile gracing his lips was a satisfied one. Last night had obviously been profitable for him, she judged. "I caught an extra shift."

She took out Candace's photograph and carefully placed it on the bar. "Did you happen to see this woman here?"

The bartender glanced at the picture. Mild interest turned to recognition. "You mean Candace Rothchild? Yeah, she was here, loud and brassy as always. But not for long," he added, looking rather disappointed. There was always a circus when Candace was around, Natalie thought. "She and the boss had at it and then he had our head of security escort her out."

She latched onto the first part of his statement. "They argued? About what?"

He shook his head. "Couldn't tell you. Too far away for anything but body language," he confessed.

"And the head of security?" she asked.

"He got her to leave."

She leaned in over the bar. "Tell me about him."

"Don't know much," the bartender admitted. "Just that his name's Matt Shaffer. Boss flew him in from L.A., where he was head of security for Montgomery Enterprises."

There was no avoiding it, she thought darkly. She was going to have to talk to Matt. The thought left her cold. "Do you know where I can find him right now?"

Kevin glanced at his watch. "He should be in his office. On the second floor, toward the rear." He gave her the numbers of the rooms where the monitors that kept watch over the casino guests as they tried their luck against the house were located.

Taking out a twenty, she placed it on the bar. "Thanks for your help."

Kevin slipped the bill into his vest pocket. "Anytime, lovely lady," he called after her. "Anytime."

She debated going up the stairs, then decided on the elevator. The car that took her up to the second floor was empty. Natalie stepped out of the elevator, looked around to get her bearings and then walked toward the rear of the floor.

"Into the Valley of Death rode the six hundred," she silently recited, digging deep for a line from a poem by Tennyson. Wrapping her hand around a brass handle, she opened one of the glass doors and walked in.

The woman whose desk was closest to the door looked up. "You can't come in here. This is a restricted area."

Natalie already had her ID in her hand and held it up. "I'm looking for Matt Shaffer," she told the woman.

God, even saying his name made her mouth go dry. She was supposed to be over him, to have moved on with her life. What happened?

The woman began to answer her. "He's—"

"Right here."

The deep voice came from behind her. Natalie felt every single nerve ending go on tactical alert at the same moment that all the hairs at the back of her neck stood up. Eight years had passed, but she would have recognized his voice anywhere.

* * * * *

Why did Matt Shaffer leave
heiress-turned-cop Natalie Rothchild?
What does he know about
the death of Natalie's twin sister?
Come and meet these two reunited lovers and
learn the secrets of the Rothchild family in
THE HEIRESS'S 2-WEEK AFFAIR
by USA TODAY bestselling author
Marie Ferrarella.
The first book in Silhouette® Romantic Suspense's
wildly romantic new continuity,
LOVE IN 60 SECONDS!
Available April 2009.

CELEBRATE
60 YEARS
OF PURE READING PLEASURE
WITH **HARLEQUIN**®!

Look for Silhouette®
Romantic Suspense in April!

Love In 60 Seconds

Bright lights. Big city. Hearts in overdrive.

Silhouette® Romantic Suspense is celebrating
Harlequin's 60th Anniversary with six stories that
promise to bring readers the glitz of Las Vegas,
the danger of revenge, the mystery of a missing
diamond, and family scandals.

**Look for the first title, *The Heiress's 2-Week Affair*
by *USA TODAY* bestselling author
Marie Ferrarella, on sale in April!**

His 7-Day Fiancée by **Gail Barrett**	May
The 9-Month Bodyguard by **Cindy Dees**	June
Prince Charming for 1 Night by **Nina Bruhns**	July
Her 24-Hour Protector by **Loreth Anne White**	August
5 minutes to Marriage by **Carla Cassidy**	September

SRS60BPA

You're invited to join our Tell Harlequin Reader Panel!

By joining our new reader panel you will:

- Receive Harlequin® books—they are FREE and yours to keep with no obligation to purchase anything!
- Participate in fun online surveys
- Exchange opinions and ideas with women just like you
- Have a say in our new book ideas and help us publish the best in women's fiction

In addition, you will have a chance to win great prizes and receive special gifts!
See Web site for details. Some conditions apply.
Space is limited.

To join, visit us at
www.TellHarlequin.com.

REQUEST YOUR FREE BOOKS!

2 FREE NOVELS PLUS 2 FREE GIFTS!

HARLEQUIN®

Super Romance®

Exciting, emotional, unexpected!

YES! Please send me 2 FREE Harlequin® Superromance® novels and my 2 FREE gifts (gifts are worth about $10). After receiving them, if I don't wish to receive any more books, I can return the shipping statement marked "cancel." If I don't cancel, I will receive 6 brand-new novels every month and be billed just $4.69 per book in the U.S. or $5.24 per book in Canada. That's a savings of close to 15% off the cover price! It's quite a bargain! Shipping and handling is just 25¢ per book*. I understand that accepting the 2 free books and gifts places me under no obligation to buy anything. I can always return a shipment and cancel at any time. Even if I never buy another book from Harlequin, the two free books and gifts are mine to keep forever.

135 HDN EEX7   336 HDN EEYK

Name	(PLEASE PRINT)	

Address		Apt. #

City	State/Prov.	Zip/Postal Code

Signature (if under 18, a parent or guardian must sign)

Mail to the **Harlequin Reader Service:**
IN U.S.A.: P.O. Box 1867, Buffalo, NY 14240-1867
IN CANADA: P.O. Box 609, Fort Erie, Ontario L2A 5X3

Not valid to current subscribers of Harlequin Superromance books.

**Are you a current subscriber of Harlequin Superromance books
and want to receive the larger-print edition?
Call 1-800-873-8635 today!**

* Terms and prices subject to change without notice. Prices do not include applicable taxes. Sales tax applicable in N.Y. Canadian residents will be charged applicable provincial taxes and GST. Offer not valid in Quebec. This offer is limited to one order per household. All orders subject to approval. Credit or debit balances in a customer's account(s) may be offset by any other outstanding balance owed by or to the customer. Please allow 4 to 6 weeks for delivery. Offer available while quantities last.

Your Privacy: Harlequin is committed to protecting your privacy. Our Privacy Policy is available online at www.eHarlequin.com or upon request from the Reader Service. From time to time we make our lists of customers available to reputable third parties who may have a product or service of interest to you. If you would prefer we not share your name and address, please check here. ☐

HSR09

Harlequin® Historical
Historical Romantic Adventure!

Undone!

THE RAKE'S INHERITED COURTESAN
Ann Lethbridge

Christopher Evernden has been assigned the unfortunate task of minding Parisian courtesan Sylvia Boisette. When Syliva sets off to find her father, Christopher has no choice but to follow and finds her kidnapped by an Irishman. Once rescued, they finally succumb to the temptation that has been brewing between them. But can they see past the limitations such a love can bring?

Available April 2009
wherever books are sold.

HARLEQUIN®
Super Romance®

COMING NEXT MONTH

Available April 14, 2009

#1554 HOME AT LAST • Margaret Watson
The McInnes Triplets
Fiona McInnes finally has the life in the Big Apple she'd always wanted. But when her father dies, she's forced to return home to help settle his estate. Now nothing's going as planned—including falling back in love with the man whose heart she shattered.

#1555 A LETTER FOR ANNIE • Laura Abbot
Going Back
Kyle Becker is over any feelings he had for Annie Greer. Then she returns to town, and suddenly he's experiencing those emotions again. But before he and Annie can share a future, Kyle must keep a promise to deliver a letter that could make her leave.

#1556 A NOT-SO-PERFECT PAST • Beth Andrews
Ex-con Dillon Ward has no illusions about who he is. Neither does his alluring landlord. But Nina Carlson needs him to repair her wrecked bakery—like, *yesterday*. And if there's one thing this struggling single mom knows, it's that nobody's perfect….

#1557 THE MISTAKE SHE MADE • Linda Style
Tori Amhearst can't keep her identity secret much longer. Ever since she brought Lincoln Crusoe home after an accident took away his memory, she's loved him on borrowed time. Because once Linc knows who she really is, she'll lose him forever.

#1558 SOMEONE LIKE HER • Janice Kay Johnson
Adrian Rutledge comes to Middleton expecting to find his estranged mother. He doesn't expect to find Lucy Peterson or a community that feels like home. Yet he gets this and more. Could it be that Lucy—and this town—is the family he's dreamed of?

#1559 THE HOUSE OF SECRETS • Elizabeth Blackwell
Everlasting Love
As soon as Alissa Franklin sees the old house, she knows it will be hers. With the help of handyman Danny—who has secrets of his own—she uncovers the truth about the original owners. But can a hundred-year-old romance inspire her to take a chance on love today?

HSRCNMBPA0309